SUMMER OF
Friends

To order additional copies of *Summer of Friends,* by Tanita Davis, call 1-800-765-6955.

Visit us at www.rhpa.org for more information on Review and Herald products.

SUMMER OF Friends

What will happen when Danni is faced with a new job, new friends, and discovering God for herself?

▲▲▲▲▲▲▲▲▲ **Tanita S. Davis** ▲▲▲▲▲▲▲▲▲

REVIEW AND HERALD® PUBLISHING ASSOCIATION
HAGERSTOWN, MD 21740

This book was
Edited by Gerald Wheeler
Designed by Patricia S. Wegh
Cover design by GenesisDesign
Cover iluustration by Linda Warner
Typeset: 11/13 Veljovic

PRINTED IN U.S.A.

03 02 01 00 99   5 4 3 2 1

R&H Cataloging Service
Davis, Tanita
    Summer of friends.

      I. Title.

                813.54

ISBN 0-8280-1292-X

Contents

"What I did last summer . . ." Danni nearly groaned as she looked at Mrs. Goin's neatly chalked white letters contrasting with the deep green of the board. Her school year was off to a typical start already. She glanced across the aisle to catch the horrified expressions of her classmates and rolled her eyes.

"Cheer up, Danni," whispered Correne, a girl sitting to her right. "At least you have something to write about this time. Didn't you have a job last summer?"

Immediately Danni felt herself smiling. A job. Not exactly the word she would have used to describe it, but yes, it was a job. Opening her binder and zipping out a piece of paper, she nodded to Correne.

"I do have something to write about this time, don't I?"

CHAPTER 1

Last Stop . . .
Camp Lupine Meadows

"*Vroooooom, . . . cough. Vrooooooooom, rattle, rattle—whoof!*" and they were off in a cloud of dust. Danni sincerely wished that Daddy would get some vehicle other than his ratty old blue pickup to chauffeur her around in. "Beggars," she reminded herself, "can't be choosy," and she knew she was certainly a beggar. No car, no money, but a job at least—a summer job she was on her way to at Lupine Meadow Camp.

As the scenery rolled by she tried to focus on the squiggle of nerves in her stomach. "Why is this freaking me out?" she asked herself. "Compared to baby-sitting one more summer for Roberta and Rod and their three kids, working in the camp kitchen should be a breeze."

Danni's father shifted gears to the sound of grinding and winced. Danni grimaced, glad to focus her thoughts elsewhere.

"Now, if we can just get there, this should be lots of fun for you," her father said. Danni laughed nervously. The truck died upon occasion—she only hoped that this was not going to be one of them! The camp director had asked all staff personnel to report to training week at 0500 hours. Danni's brother Bart felt he had to explain to her that in military time that just meant 5:00 a.m.

"How much longer, Dad?" she asked before she could stop herself. She chuckled, and her father grinned.

"The drive shouldn't take us more than about three hours, barring road conditions and the truck. Why don't you try to take a little nap or something? It'll sure beat worrying about what you're going to do when you get there."

She stared at him. As if she was going to sleep through what could be the beginning of the most exciting summer of her 16 years! Still, the black ribbon of freeway was boring her to death already. Maybe she'd take just a little catnap now . . .

When Danni woke up, the first thing she noticed was the dimness outside. Startled, she jerked up and peered around. They were winding their way through a forest. Occasional logging trucks whizzed by at alarming speeds. High above, through the waving greenery, Danni could see that the sun was still shining. Ribbons of light sliced through the branches of massive redwoods and quivered on fernlike plants below.

"Real pretty, isn't it?" Her father smiled at her bleary-eyed gazing. "We're about a half hour from the camp. I was just about to wake you up, girl." He touched her arm with a gentle, calloused hand.

Danni sat up and wiped her creased face with her hand. Her fingers twitched as she imagined holding a pencil and sketching the trees. Smoothing tendrils of light brown hair away from her face, she said, "We're definitely not in Lakeland anymore, are we, Dad?"

He chuckled. Danni concentrated on making conversation with her father about calling home, writing, and using her ATM card. As they rattled over a cattle guard and around a corner they came face-to-face with a huge wooden sign that read "Lupine Meadow Camp" and a green arrow urging them onward. Danni's arms tingled with goose bumps. She was really finally there.

"0500 hours."

"Are we really going to have to hear this military time junk all summer long?" a girl with a brushfire of red hair swirling around her face groaned.

"Who knows. Macomber is already making noises about KP for those who don't make their appointments on time, so we'd better hustle," replied a long-legged girl with short black hair.

"*I* don't intend to spend more time in the kitchen this summer than I have to," the redhead retorted.

From the little cave she'd created on her bottom bunk, Danni watched the girls with interest. She had met "Macomber" and thought that the girls' director was going to be a friend, even if she did have a reputation for handing out pretty tough punishments for lateness. As for spending time in the kitchen—well, that's what she was here for.

Surrounded by her possessions—a battered black footlocker at the end of her bunk, a pair of scuffed cowboy boots, and a box of sketch pads and pencils—Danni didn't feel lonely. For a moment as Daddy had rattled off down the road she had fought a constriction in her throat, but as she had entered the quarters for the staff, half a dozen girls had greeted her warmly, and several had introduced themselves. She had even found a girl she knew from her youth group at church—Roseanne Birton. Still, Danni hung back, watching.

The side entrance to the girls' quarters opened, and a buxom older girl stepped through. From the clipboard tucked under her arm, and her Lupine Meadow Staff shirt, Danni guessed that she was someone official. As she walked into the room she bellowed, "Five 'til five, girls. Move it out!" Then, scowling at her clipboard, she called out, "Dannielle Mallory?"

With a start Danni untangled herself from her bunk and stood in the aisle. The girl waved her over, and as Danni drew closer to her, she realized that the other girl stood no taller than about 5' 2". Still, confidence radiated from her smile. Danni straightened self-consciously, noticing the redheaded girl lingering near the door.

"Hi, Dannielle." The girl thrust out a small, brown-skinned hand. "I'm Eva Davies, and I'm the program director here."

For a moment Danni imagined Eva managing a room full of computers. Her bewilderment was short-lived, as the girl continued, "All of the campfire programs and plays and things are my responsibility. It looks like I'm going to be missing my assistant for at least half of the summer, and I thought since you had done some drama work at your school last year you could fill in for now until we found somebody. The kitchen has enough staff right now so that they won't miss you. Sound reasonable?" Her large brown eyes focused sharply on Danni.

"Um-yeah," Danni blurted, feeling stupid at her stumbling. "Great. Thanks."

Another brilliant smile from Eva rewarded her. "Thank you, Dannielle. Let's walk up now for the assembly with Director Ahrens, then afterward I'll show you where the program office is, and we'll go from there."

She turned and swept briskly from the room, evidently expecting Danni to follow. Danni stumbled after her, feeling excitement flood through her. From kitchen girl to program assistant! Maybe it would be a killer summer after all!

CHAPTER 2

Into the "Wild Blue Yonder"

Director Ahrens was a massive man, his face a wealth of weather wrinkles and smiles. A shock wave of black hair stood crisply at attention atop his shining head, and his eyes were nearly lost in a squinched fold of cheek when he smiled. His small wife, standing next to him, contrasted with his bold military bearing. Her salt-and-pepper hair was wound in a thick braid around her head, and she smiled up at her husband who was welcoming the staff. He had a booming voice, and seemed to take great delight in repeating himself.

Just now he was rumbling, "A pleasure to have you all, yes, a pleasure to have you all. Staffing is what makes Lupine Meadow great. Each and every one of you was handpicked, yes, handpicked from your high school or church group, because here at Lupine Meadow we take only the best, we take *only* the best."

Danni found herself caught between an alarmed frown and a giggle. He sounded silly, raving on like that. She glanced at Eva, and noted the long-suffering expression on her face. "Is he always like this?" Danni whispered.

Eva made a gloomy face and replied in a low voice, "Only on days that end in y."

Biting her lips and staring straight ahead, Danni

willed the laughter bubbling up in her to go away.

With a smile Eva added, "Actually, he's not so bad after the first week. By then we're all too busy to stand around jawing all day. His wife is great, though. You'll like her."

Danni had to agree with the "busy" part. At the beginning of Mr. Ahrens' presentation, he had handed around the weekly camp schedule that they would follow when the campers arrived. Every minute seemed bursting with activities and classes from breakfast 'til dark. Danni had scanned the list until she had noted the one hour that she was looking for—Quiet Hour. From 1:00-2:00 p.m. the entire camp shut down for an hour of quiet letter writing, siestas, and other peaceful activities. Danni had already decided that was the time that she would look forward to most every day.

Mr. Ahrens finally wound down his speech. He had summoned the cooks out so that the other staff could applaud them, and finally requested somebody to say grace. A tall young man with wide shoulders and a shock of wavy black hair falling over his forehead rose and bowed his head. Danni stared at him, noting the dark feathering of his long lashes and the precise line of his nose. She glanced at Eva and noticed with some surprise that she was peeking too.

Supper was a simple affair of oniony burgers and crisp salty fries. Fresh strawberry shortcake rounded out the meal, and Danni pushed herself away from the table with a groan. Eva was finishing an animated conversation with the dark-haired girl next to her, exclaiming, "I have no idea what you're talking about!"

The girl shook her finger at Eva in mock scolding. "Just you wait, Evita," she taunted.

Looking more distressed than amused, Eva shook her head and rose from the table. "Come on, Dannielle,

14

we've got to get started," she called, dumping her tray and stacking it on the conveyer belt.

Danni followed suit and trailed behind her as they left the cafeteria. As she stood on the porch, the beauty of the Lupine Meadow before her once again silenced her. Acre after acre unfolded in long grassy stretches, dotted by orange poppies and the blue lupine flowers the camp was famous for. To the east, a pond glowed like a green eye in the lower meadow, while to the west, towering pines and redwoods darkened the horizon. Danni stood still for a moment to drink in the meadow's beauty. Eva was smiling back at her.

"Take advantage of the view, Dannielle," Eva said softly. "Most staff forget it's there by the second week. If you can keep looking at it all summer long, you can keep focused when things get hectic. Believe me, you'll need this." Eva turned toward the faraway pond and took a deep breath. "You can ignore the whole world if you just have something positive to focus on."

Danni thought it a strange statement, and was prepared to say so when she saw Eva straighten up and turn away briskly. Trotting to catch up, she panted, "So where are we headed?"

"The program office is in the basement of the old Lupine headquarters where the camp offices are set up. Didn't you take a tour of everything when you registered?"

"No, not really. It was a long drive for us, and Daddy was in a hurry to be home before dark." At Eva's questioning glance she added, "Kind of a junker car." The older girl nodded understandingly.

"Well, if you're up for a short hike, I'll show you what I can before campfire," the program director offered.

"Super!" Danni beamed.

A long wooden bridge crossed the lowest part of the

meadow. Eva had explained that the grassland in some parts of the meadow area was protected land, and that the bridge had been built to preserve the native flora and fauna of the area. Silvery fish darted in a small stream that trickled beneath the bridge. A baseball diamond to their left was filled with staff who yelled to Eva and Danni to join them in a game, but Eva shook her head and waved at them. The two of them continued on.

A long hill followed the bridge. "At the end of this monstrosity of a hill is our nature center," Eva puffed. "Pretty new, it has state-of-the-art everything. It has a really neat telescope tower that you'll have to come and visit some night—before curfew." She winked.

At the nature center a seven-foot-tall stuffed bear greeted them at the entrance.

"Charming fellow, isn't he?"

"Where did they get him?" Danni asked a little uneasily.

"Cheer up, dear environmentalist," Eva teased her. "Nobody hunts at Lupine Meadows. This fellow probably died comfortably of old age and was donated to us from a zoo."

"Oh." Danni felt silly.

Eva checked her watch. "We'd probably better hurry. When you have a little free time tomorrow you can check this place out in detail. Right now I want you to know where the arts and crafts building is, and then we need to get jackets and get bug-proofed for campfire."

Leaving the nature center, they continued up hill. At a clearing in the woods they turned down a graveled road that eventually became paved. Suddenly Danni realized that they were walking on the road she and her father had driven in on. They passed log cabins that had been mostly camouflaged from the car window. Eva veered sharply from the paved road and walked up a dirt track lined by logs.

"And yes, in response to your unspoken question,

everything is on a hill here," she huffed. Danni laughed.

They stopped at the crest of the small hill as Eva pointed. "This is the arts and crafts building, and to the left over there is the machine shop. The little brick outbuilding to your right houses a kiln. And this"—she broke off as a door opened—"is Ooooold Glory!" she finished in a circus hawker voice.

A Latina girl she had seen at supper stood framed in the doorway. Her dark hair and sparkling brown eyes perfectly complimented her mischievously quirked lips. "Quiet, Evita," she warned, "or . . ." She made threatening gestures with a cup of water she held in her hands.

"Danni, this is Gloria Rodriguez, my roommate and the camp nurse," Eva said cheerfully. "When she's not pursuing doctors, she's up here working with oil painting, her other consuming passion."

"Speaking of consuming passions . . ." Gloria muttered.

"Glory," Eva began severely.

The other girl merely wiggled her eyebrows suggestively.

"Unfortunately the arts and crafts director isn't here," Eva continued, pointedly ignoring the other girl.

"Ah, but he is," Gloria chortled. "And in prime form."

"Gloria, would you stop it!" Eva snapped.

Darting over to Danni, Gloria grabbed her arm. "Come and see this," she hissed, and pulled her around the back of the building.

A little ways away from the crafts building a man sat in intense concentration before a pottery wheel. Shirtless and splattered with clay, he patiently coaxed a pitcher from a cylindrical blob that rose and fell as it spun. Although a bandanna covered his dark hair, a stubborn lock straggled across his forehead, and Danni recognized him as the guy who had asked the blessing for dinner. She stared at his muscular arms. He certainly looked a lot different without a shirt on.

"Hey, Da*vid*, I'm going down now," Gloria called, using the Spanish emphasis on the last syllable of his name.

He replied in Spanish, something fluid and unintelligible, then glanced up, noticing Danni. "Oh!" he blurted, startled. With dirty hands he reached for his shirt, slung clumsily over the end of his workbench. Glancing at his hands, he grimaced, stopping the wheel. As he stood up, Eva rounded the corner.

"Hi!" he stuttered, quickly wiping his hands and pulling his shirt over his head, at the same time blushing from the roots of his hair. Danni was surprised. She wondered if he just didn't like visitors and if Gloria had done this to him on purpose.

Sticking out a clay-smeared hand, he introduced himself. "I'm David Taylor. I saw you in the mess hall."

Immediately Danni took his hand, noting the deep dimples his smile produced. "Danni Mallory. You're the director up here?"

"Yeah, me and Gloria when she'll help me." The Hispanic girl stuck her tongue out at him. "Actually I have two part-time assistants. Gloria, when she doesn't have to be slapping Band-Aids on people, and the director's wife, Marge Ahrens. So you're working in the kitchen this summer?"

"Does it show?" Danni asked incredulously.

Gloria chuckled. "Danni, if you're under 18 you can't be a counselor, so the kitchen or general staff assistant is usually all you can be at your age."

Eva joined in the conversation. "Actually, she's my assistant."

"You get two assistants this year?" David exclaimed. "Great! Maybe I'll see a lot more of you around here." Then he turned his dimples on her.

She smiled wryly. "I wish. Actually I have one assistant, and who knows if or when Jeannie is showing up. She got involved with her schoolwork to the point of running off with her professor at the end of the semester. They're probably hitched by now."

Gloria made a face. "Eeeew. And his *hair* was thinning."

David, Eva, and Danni laughed.

"Nothing like a little substance in a woman," Eva chortled.

"I am verrry substantial," Glory protested, theatrically rolling her r's. "It's just that I like my men fully furred!"

"Oh, please," Eva groaned.

David glanced at his watch. "I hate to change the subject after such a revealing glimpse into the nature of women, but we'd all better get going. I have to change out of this"—he gestured at his spattered person—"and there's an executive meeting before campfire, so I've gotta jet."

He turned to Danni. "Hope to see a lot more of you, friend, and your sidekick here." He nodded to Eva and then turned away.

"I'll lock up, David," Gloria said to his retreating form.

"Thanks." He waved and disappeared down a trail through the woods.

"Well, 'sidekick,' shall we go?" Danni asked.

"He's cute, isn't he?" Eva said distractedly, appearing not to have heard.

"Well, yeah—and isn't that a cool pot he was throwing? That's what I'd like to do someday," Danni replied enthusiastically.

Gloria laughed. "Oh good, another artiste. We're gonna have a ball up here this summer, *hermanas* (sisters)."

"Yeah. You, me, and the mad artists here," Eva grinned sarcastically.

"Oh, just admit it, girl, you're hopelessly devoted . . ." Gloria darted out of Eva's reach.

"Gloria, if you can't just admit that you're the one

he's interested in, it's beyond me to try to tell you."

"Eva, he's not my type—I like dangerous men."

"*Hello*, he drives a motorcycle!"

"Not dangerous enough."

"Yeah, you prefer old professors."

"Yuck, can you believe Jeannie's actually doing that?"

"Actually, I'm really concerned. She wasn't attending a Christian college this last year, was she?"

"I don't think so. Really, this just wasn't her style. Have you talked to her at all?"

The conversation wound on, and Danni just listened, absorbing it all, and kept her thoughts to herself.

"Staff Week sure is a lot of work," a girl named Darla complained as the camp staff got ready for bed.

"Ha! Just wait until tomorrow," Lena, a tall brunette, replied, stretching out on her bed. "I hear that we're going to be doing some sort of team building exercises. Last summer we ran all over the place. Mr. Ahrens can sure wear you out."

Lying on her bunk, Danni listened apprehensively. Screwing up her courage, she sat up and addressed the dark-haired girl. "Lena, how long have you been working here?"

Heads turned her direction. "Two summers," Lena replied in a friendly fashion. "Why?"

"Well," Danni gulped, feeling her face redden, "I kind of just want to know what kind of things we'll be doing tomorrow, if you know. I mean, I'm not the greatest at sports."

The redheaded girl in the bunk next to Lena said, "I hear you're going to be in programming instead of in the kitchen. Why don't you ask that Eva girl?"

Lena waved a hand to silence her. "I think it's a good question. Dannielle, it's not 'team' like as in a baseball team—it's team stuff like working together to build something, or being a human wall to reach the top of something. It's like a challenge kind of thing. Everyone is supposed to do their own personal best."

The brown-eyed Darla pulled back her hair into a ponytail. "Lena, you sound just like Ahrens, you know that?"

Lena threw a pillow at her.

"Well, thanks." Danni lay back on her bunk, feeling a little less worried.

"Don't worry," Darla said as the lights went out, "I'm sure you won't be the only one who doesn't know what they're doing."

"We have to *what?*" Katherine Armstrong whined. The light wind teased her mane of coppery hair around her face as she stared incredulously at the slip of paper in her hand.

Danni took a cautious step closer to peer at the sheet. "Well, it looks like we're being sent on a treasure hunt," she said warily. She glanced up at the girl most of the staff called Kat. "And it looks like we've been chosen as the group leaders." Shyly she glanced at the circle of expectant faces.

Kat balled up the paper with a furious gesture. "I can read," she snapped. She tossed back her hair and fixed the small group with a dark look. "OK, you guys. I'm in charge here, and this is how we're going to do this. We are supposed to be getting something from each spot we go to, and we're being timed. So we're going to split up" — she divided the group in half with the wave of a hand— "and find our stuff and be done with it. OK?"

Danni's heart sank. "Actually, Kat?" she heard a timid voice that didn't sound like her own.

"What?" The other girl fixed her with a steely gaze.

"Well, according to what I read, we're supposed to stay

together. If we find the clues out of order, they won't make sense, and we won't find whatever it is that we're supposed to be getting. I really don't think we should split up."

"Thank you, Danni," Kat said sarcastically. "We're being *timed*, do you understand that? It's a waste of time if we all stay together."

"Come on, Kat, it's supposed to be about teamwork," a tall boy with blue eyes spoke from beneath his baseball cap. Danni recognized him as Roseanne Birton's twin brother, Kevin.

"That's supposed to be the point," agreed a graceful-looking girl with light brown hair.

"Well," Danni squared her shoulders, not looking at Kat, "let's get started, then."

"The first clue should be on the sheet," a boy named Jose advised them.

Kat uncrumpled the paper sullenly. "This is a total waste of time," she repeated. "The first place this says to go is to the old Lupine House, which is on the east end of the meadow, on the way down to the Cowboy Camp. And our clue is 'Has your life lost its savor? Here's something to add a little flavor.' Hmm." Kat looked intrigued in spite of herself.

"Well, let's go!" the sturdy-looking girl standing closest to Danni said. She skipped on ahead.

"You won't go wrong if you let Tina lead us." The graceful-looking girl was walking next to Danni. "She knows this camp like the back of her hand because she was a camper here for years."

Danni would have responded, but Kat yelled, "Why are you guys walking? *Run!* We're being *timed!*"

With a groan Danni broke into a hasty trot to catch up with her coleader.

At the Lupine House the group searched vainly for the next clue. "There aren't even any plants here that you can cook with to add flavor to anything," Tina complained, looking glum.

"Do you think it's got something to do with the horse trough?" Jose asked. They all stared at the dark water.

"Ugh," Danni shuddered. "That water would flavor things, all right, but not something I'd eat. What's that rock there?"

"A salt lick." Kevin nudged it with his boot. "It's for the cattle." He stopped suddenly.

"Kevin? What are you thinking?" The brownheaded Glenda looked from Kevin to the salt block, then dropped to her knees and tried to turn it over. "Help me, you guys," she called out, scrabbling in the dirt.

Danni was on her knees immediately, with Kevin and a girl named Suzanne pulling at the top of the large salt block.

"Here's something." Glenda smoothed out a smudged scrap of paper.

" 'Go west, young friends, and circle the wagons'?" Jose sounded unsure. "Does that mean we go to Cowboy Camp or the Native Village?"

"Well, technically, west is the way we just came from," Kevin frowned. "What do you think, Joe?" He turned to the quiet Asian boy next to him.

Joe shrugged. "Doesn't 'circle the wagons' mean to make a circle and look out for danger? The danger usually came from the Native Americans—in frontier times."

"And," Danni said slowly, "when they went west, they went into Indian country."

"That's got to be the dumbest thing I've ever heard," Kat groaned.

"Well, it is quite a stretch," Jose agreed. "But I'm willing to take a gamble."

"Me too," Glenda said firmly.

"Let's start running." Tina took off.

"Wait!" Joe called after her. "How are we supposed to circle our wagons when we're running?"

Danni laughed. "You tell me," she said, and jogged after her.

Kevin met Danni at the top of the hill. "How long have you been up here?" he asked enviously as he flopped down on the ground.

"Not long enough," she panted, rubbing the stitch in her side. "I think this is the best place to let everybody catch up and take a breather. I don't want to go into the village by myself . . . something tells me that we may have to circle up pretty soon. Hear that?"

They paused for a moment to listen to the deep throb of drums drifting on the wind. Kevin nodded. "Somebody's up here."

"I guess they'll give us our next clue." They sat quietly for a moment.

"Did you guys hear the drums?" Tina dropped to the ground next to them.

"There are people up here!" Suzanne exclaimed, rounding the last bend.

Joe, Glenda, Jose, and Kat arrived in quick succession. Kat looked exhausted. Dirt smudging her cheek, she leaned against a tree and closed her eyes.

"I think we should stay together from now on," Danni said. "We don't know who's up here with these drums, and they might try to keep us from finding whatever we're supposed to find. Does anybody have any ideas of what to do next?"

"I need a drink of water," Kat coughed.

"There's a fountain up at the village," Tina reassured her.

"Well, let's go." Kat pushed off from the tree and staggered down the trail. The others crowded after her.

The camp looked abandoned. A massive white tepee decorated with running buffaloes and arrows dominated one side of a huge fire pit. Smaller tepees surrounded it.

"This place is really neat!" Danni looked around, wide-eyed.

"It's filthy," Kat frowned. She felt better after her drink.

"Where do we start?" Suzanne wanted to know.

A bloodcurdling war whoop followed her words. Danni jumped, and Joe cried, "Circle the wagons!"

Danni and Kat grabbed each other to finish the circle. Then from nowhere, an arrow skittered to the ground in front of them.

"Run!" Suzanne howled.

"Wait!" Tina cried, picking up the arrow. Attached to its base was a slip of white paper. Opening it, she read, "Your party is under attack. The only way to safety is behind the wall of your fort. You must climb over the wall to escape. You may not go around the wall."

"What wall?" Glenda wrinkled up her nose.

"I think we'd better follow the trail," Tina advised.

"We're supposed to go over *this?*" Danni looked up at the wooden wall. "This wall's at least 14 feet tall!"

"I can get up it," Kevin offered. He took a running start and scrambled up the obstacle, gripping for handholds and footholds. After getting a leg over the top, he stopped for a moment to get a breath.

"I can't do that," Suzanne said quietly.

"Wait a minute," Jose said. "Don't panic yet. I have an idea."

He wrestled a rotting log over to the base of the wall. Danni, catching his thought, stood on it to test its strength. Jose stood on the end nearest Kevin and looked up at the taller boy. "OK. Do you think you could help me get up there?"

"I'll do my best," Kevin replied, reaching down an arm.

Jose pulled himself up, grunting. He flung his leg

over the top of the wall and hung there for a moment. Then Kevin boosted him over. "I made it!" Jose was pleased with himself.

"How are you going to get down?" Kat asked in a small voice.

"I'm not—at least not yet. Kevin and I can pull everybody over."

"Not me," Suzanne muttered, blushing to the roots of her hair. "I'm too heavy."

"No, you're not," Danni said. "We'll help you from down here if you can't get started. We can do this." She looked around. "Who wants to go first?"

"I will," Kat declared. She jumped onto the log and held up her arms. Kevin grabbed one, and Jose the other. In a remarkably short time, she sat atop the wall. Then, with a panicked expression, she dropped down the other side.

"Are you OK?" Danni yelled.

Glenda pulled a two-way radio out of her jacket pocket. Danni looked at her in surprise.

"I'm fine," Kat replied. "It's a long way down, though. Somebody needs to come over and help me get people down."

"I'm next," Joe said.

"Hey," Danni touched Glenda's arm. "Why do you have a radio?"

"Just in case anyone gets hurt," the other girl replied, shoving it back into her pocket. "There's one person in each group with one. We're supposed to be building team spirit here, not killing ourselves in the woods." She grinned at Danni.

"Well, does that mean that you know what we're supposed to be finding?"

"No. I just know where we are and how to call in, that's all."

"Good." Now Danni smiled. "It's more fun that way."

"We need the next person," Kat yelled. "Remember, we're being *timed!*"

"C'mon, Suzie," Tina said cheerfully. "You're next."

CHAPTER 3

Sincerely . . .

June 13 . . . Friday

Dear Daddy, Betti, and the animal who calls himself my older brother:

OK, guys—I'm ready. I have my camp shirts, my cowboy hat and duds for rodeo night, my headdress for Native American night, my clown outfit for carnival night, and my swimsuit for my day off. Can you believe how much they do with these kids every day? I can't believe that week after next I'll get a chance to do something with the kids. Some of the staff who aren't counselors get to give the counselors a break during Brownie camp by staying with them during the Quiet Hour—so the counselors can get some real sleep.

I can't believe how lucky I am that Eva picked me to be her assistant! And all I did for the drama department was do backgrounds and play with makeup and stuff. I can't believe I'm getting paid for that same thing here. In the mornings we have staff meeting before the kids get up. The executive staff take turns giving talks that motivate us into doing really well with the campers. Next everybody tells about what the activities are for the day, and then coordinates with everybody else to do them. (OK, I am using "everybody" a little much. But that's how it is!) Eva and I plan camp councils, campfires, and all of the games and activities everybody does when they're not taking classes such as horseback riding or swimming lessons or Colonial America in which they make candles, Native American Lore in which they make dreamcatchers, or Mountain Lore in which they rappel off of mountains and identify rocks and stuff. Of course, that's not to mention my favorite thing—the A&C—that's arts and crafts. I still haven't spent too much time there because Eva never seems to want to go, so I go with Gloria—she's the nurse, did I tell you that?—to help out. David Taylor is really nice, and he's helping me learn more about pottery. I get a little time to sketch every day—and there's a photography class and a darkroom here that I'll help to pick color slides from for the Saturday night slide show. Cool, huh?

Betti, Dad, thanks for letting me come. For the most part, I'm having a really good time. Only a couple of things kind of bug me . . . I had to do an activity with a girl named Kat, and I don't think she likes me. We were group leaders for a team-building exercise, and we came in second place. Kat thinks it's my fault. I've tried to tell her I'm sorry, but . . . The funny thing is that we never found what it was we were supposed to find—at least I didn't think so. When we got back, Mr. A. told us we were supposed to have found the spirit of teamwork. I'm still not sure Kat has it!

Anyway, there's "disABILITY" camp next week. In 10 minutes I have to go back to work to help Eva get ready for it. How can we plan skits and stuff for people who are blind and deaf and stuff? Some of them even have mental disabilities. On Sunday at staff meeting we're supposed to experience being handicapped . . . which sounds scary. Lena, one of the girls who works in laundry, was here last summer, and says that "disABILITY week" is one of the hardest in the whole summer.

Oops—Eva's here early, and I had better get.

P.S. Are you still coming for the Fourth of July? I'll make sure that's my day off.

Your everloving daughter,

Danni

CHAPTER 4

Mari

Danni's mouth watered as she smelled oregano and garlic. Carefully she put out her hands to feel for her plate, patting beside her plate to discover where her fork was. She fumbled for its handle.

"OK, D, spaghetti at three o'clock, salad at six o'clock, and green beans at . . . mmm, maybe 11:45ish." Gloria's voice had a teasing note to it.

"Oh, my, I *hate* this," moaned a voice to Danni's left.

"Think about if it were permanent," another voice commented.

Danni bit her lip, determined to master this little exercise if it was the last thing that she ever did.

"How are we doing here?" boomed a voice above her.

Danni gulped as she recognized Mr. Ahrens' voice. "Just fine, sir," she replied in a strangled voice, losing track of her fork.

"Good for you, young lady, good for you," he rumbled, patting her smartly on the shoulder.

Danni sighed and tried to recover her utensil.

"Here, let me," she heard Eva's voice, and felt her fork pressed into her hand. "Most nonsighted people don't have to put up with Mr. Ahrens, so you're at an unfair disadvantage."

Danni laughed as she again tried to wind her spaghetti on her fork and carry it to her mouth. She made it—with only minor spillage.

"Looking good, Danni," said a familiar voice. "Think you can show me the ropes on this one?"

"Hi, David," Danni smiled in his general direction. "I'd show you the ropes if I could find them. Are you disabled too?"

"No, only the first-year staff get to be disabled. The rest of us get to lead you and assist you. My first year I had my right arm and hand taped down as if I were an amputee. It really makes you think about what you have when you lose something."

A chair creaked nearby and Danni smelled a whiff of cologne. She leaned forward and sniffed, amazed at how her other senses had sharpened. "David, I can smell you!" she exclaimed.

Gloria let out a whoop of laughter and pounded her fists on the table. Even Eva, who was usually so reserved around David, let out a cackle. Danni wished she could sink through the floor.

"David, I told you to shower before you came down to dinner," Gloria howled.

"That's not what I meant!" Danni wailed.

"I know what you mean even if this nut doesn't," David replied with a smile in his voice. "It is pretty weird when all of a sudden you can hear a pin drop and smell and feel stuff you usually never notice. That's what we do it for, so we know a little of what it's like to be in somebody else's place, and realize how much we are blessed." He patted her shoulder.

"You can probably take it off now so you can eat before your dinner gets too cold," Gloria told her.

Danni clawed off the eye patches with relief and blinked her eyes in the sudden brightness. "Much better," she muttered, reaching for her French bread.

Later that evening as Danni prepared for bed in the staff quarters, she heard murmured conversations all around her about the "disABILITY" experience.

"It's just way . . . gross," Kat, the redheaded girl, said scornfully. "They can't even find their own mouths, and they just spill food all over everywhere—already chewed food and everything."

Suzanne nodded, flipping her dark tassel of hair. "A whole week of this! I'm not eating anything." She scowled.

"What do you think, Darla? You were here last summer," Lena asked. "Didn't you just think it was the hardest week of the summer?"

"No," Darla replied.

"What?" Kat shrilled. "They all didn't just gross you out?"

"No," Darla said, a little more sharply this time. Danni heard the tension in her voice.

"Well, what's the matter with you, anyway?" Kat snapped. "You're awfully cranky tonight."

"That's because I'm tired of hearing you talk," Darla snarled, then stomped into the bathroom.

A shocked silence hung in the room.

"I think she's upset because her sister's blind," Danni began slowly. "I saw her when she came up, and they look just alike. She's really pretty, and you can hardly tell that she's blind because she uses her cane so well, and—"

"So, why didn't you say something, stupid?" Kat demanded. She flung herself onto her bed. Suzanne backed toward her bunk. Lena gave Danni an apologetic look and hurried into the bathroom after Darla.

Bewildered, Danni crawled back into her bunk.

Sunday morning was warm and windy. Danni stood

nervously as the orange-and-silver bus pulled up and campers began to slowly emerge. Some were chatting loudly as they stepped out onto the bus lot. Others looked frightened. Danni noticed that one of the last campers out was a fragile looking blond girl with short cropped hair and braces on her legs. She appeared close to Danni's age. What was most noticeable about her was that she stubbornly refused any assistance as she made her way out of the bus and carefully across the parking lot toward the lodge.

Counselors and other staff walked by with blind campers steadying themselves on either arm. Some of the more mobile campers assisted friends of theirs who had a harder time getting around. Danni looked for someone to assist. Her eyes lighted on the girl with the leg braces, still slowly making her way toward her destination. "Hi," she said cautiously to the girl.

The girl grunted and continued walking.

"I-I'm really glad that it isn't any hotter yet today. How was the trip up here?"

Silence.

Again Danni tried to make conversation. "Where did you come from?"

"Fresno."

Danni blinked. "That must have been like a six-hour drive! Do you do this every year?"

"Nope. First time."

Gratefully Danni leapt on this fact. "Oh, you must be so excited! This is my first summer too, and there's so much stuff to do here that you won't be sorry you came. You'll have a lot of fun."

The girl gave Danni an angry stare. "Look. I've been to handicapped camps before. This one is going to be boring, just like all of the others. I don't need you to talk to me 'cause you feel sorry for me, OK? So—" Turning away, she continued to wend her way slowly into the lodge.

Danni felt as if she had been doused in ice water. Her head was ringing and her face was tight and hot with embarrassment and anger. Tears pricked her eyelids, and she swallowed hard for a moment. Never had anyone so utterly rejected her.

Taking a deep breath, she calmed herself and decided that she was too old to cry about some girl not liking her. "Please give me patience, God," she muttered grimly. Deciding to have the last word, she followed the girl a few steps farther.

"I was just trying to make conversation," she called loudly to the girl's retreating back, "and I just wanted to make you feel welcome here. My name's Danni. If you ever need anything, just ask."

The girl shrugged and continued walking.

"Good job," a voice said softly next to her ear. Danni turned and saw blue-eyed Mrs. Ahrens standing close beside her.

"A lot of these people feel very hostile and angry about being disabled. Some of them have cataracts and glaucoma and know that they will see and do less and less every year. Others of them are disabled because of accidents, or birth defects, and can't see that there is ever any hope for them." She slipped a comforting arm around Danni.

"The best we can do for any of our guests this week is to be normal and friendly, and some of them like Mari will come around. Most of them will have a really good time, you'll see."

"I hope so," Danni muttered, feeling somewhat better.

"So you've met Mari too," Eva said dryly after hearing Danni's tale. "Every camp has someone like her—don't take it too personally."

"But why is she here if she doesn't feel like being

here?" Danni scraped her chair back from her desk and flopped down dejectedly.

"Because, O mournful one, her parents probably sent her here in hope that she would have a good time, and that's what we're going to give her."

"Whether she wants it or not," Danni muttered darkly.

"No, my dear, not 'whether she wants it or not,'" Eva laughed. "Everybody has the choice to participate in the fun—or not. She has to choose to have fun. All we can do is make sure that the fun is there to have."

Eva smiled at Danni's mutinous expression and added, "Work is the best cure for a cranky person, girl, so let's hit it!"

It turned out that Danni didn't have time to think about Mari again until Monday morning. At staff meeting Bill Wright, who was an assistant at the nature center, gave a devotional talk on how some people were like turtles and some were like porcupines—but all of those natural defenses were just that—defenses.

"You might not think that you could cuddle up with a porcupine," Bill concluded, his brown eyes serious behind his silver-framed glasses, "but when they put their quills down, they're a whole different animal."

"I'd like to see what's beneath Mari Burtz's quills," Terri, a counselor, interjected. "Last night when our cabin came by to say goodnight to Christine's, she was pretty nasty. How are you handling her, Christine?"

"Well . . ." Christine hesitated, raking her hands through her brown hair.

"Is something else wrong?" Lee Macomber, the girls' director, asked, smiling sympathetically.

"Well," Christine said again, "she's already made it pretty clear that she doesn't think that I'm worth talking to, and she's already hurt the feelings of a couple of my younger campers who usually like everyone, and she's already told me this morning that she's not going to do anything today. What can I do, Lee?"

Lee glanced at her watch, then at Director Ahrens. "Let's end our meeting right now with prayer, and unless anybody else has any new business, Christine, I'll meet with you directly afterward."

Mr. Ahrens nodded, and Macomber led the staff in a short prayer.

"All right," Mr. Ahrens said afterward. "Go get 'em, everybody! And have a great day!" Then he turned. "Now, Christine, why don't you come right over here . . ."

Christine, Lee, and Mr. Ahrens were blocked from Danni's view as staff rose and milled out of the lodge. Danni stood and stretched, wishing she could hear what advice Macomber had about Mari, then made her way back to the staff quarters to prepare for breakfast. On the way she fell in step with blond-haired Roseanne Birton, and her brother, Kevin, who had been in her team-building group.

"Hey, guys," she greeted them.

"Hey." Kevin looked up from under his customary baseball cap.

"How are things going in programming?" Roseanne asked eagerly.

"Just great. I really like working with Eva."

Kevin waved goodbye as he turned off toward the guys' quarters.

"Honestly?" Roseanne continued. "I heard that Eva is really kind of a witch. Kat Armstrong says she's on a huge power trip, and she's only 20. I heard that she got this job only because she is dating the horsemanship director, and the Ahrenses really like him."

Shocked, Danni stood still for a moment, wondering what to say. "I really don't know anything except that

Eva's really nice, and I'm glad I get to work with her,"
she said slowly. Roseanne nodded. "I wouldn't take everything Kat says as . . . well, I think you should get to
know people for yourself, you know what I mean?" She
looked hopefully at Roseanne.

Roseanne shrugged. "Kat's always saying stuff. I figured that Eva was pretty cool, or you wouldn't hang out
with her, you know?"

"Yeah," Danni agreed.

"Don't worry," Roseanne reassured her, "I know better than to believe all the gossip I hear."

Danni shrugged uneasily as they entered the staff
quarters in silence.

After Camp Council that morning, Danni assisted a
cabin of girls down to the pond to canoe. Already the
morning was warm and sunny, with hardly a hint of a
breeze. On the way past the staff quarters, Danni
stopped by to retrieve her sketch pad and a handful of
colored pencils.

"What are you going to draw?" a 9-year-old girl named
Tanya asked her wistfully, fingering Danni's pencils.

"Just you guys, and the pond, and the sunshine, and
stuff," Danni replied enthusiastically.

"I wish I could draw," Tanya said sadly.

"Why can't you?"

"Well, because all of my stuff doesn't look right, and
. . ." Tanya pushed up her thick glasses and waved her
hands in frustration.

Danni caught a flying hand in her own. "Tanya, it
doesn't have to look like anything anybody else does. If
all of our artwork looked the same, wouldn't it be boring? When you go to the arts and crafts building this afternoon, just make sure you have fun inventing your
very own original thing, and I bet it'll look great."

The younger girl smiled shyly. "If you say so," she said.

Moths and gauzy-winged dragonflies fluttered around the pond. A group of girls were already paddling with great splashes across the pond's smooth surface. Danni recognized Christine standing resignedly next to the bowed blondheaded figure of Mari. She hurried over.

"Isn't it pretty out here, Christine? I just love the pond. Are you going to go in a canoe with your girls?"

"As soon as my cocounselor comes back to keep Mari here company. What are you doing down here?"

"I just came down here to help out with Jenny's cabin. I'd like to keep Mari company if you'd like to go and join your cabin."

Christine's eyes lit up. "Would you like to?" she asked with a cautious glance at Mari.

"Oh, sure. I'm just going to be sketching here for a while."

"Well, OK . . . Mari, let me know if you change your mind, and I'll trade out with you, OK?"

The camper ignored her. With a shrug Christine stepped down to the dock. Danni pulled out her pencils and squinted at the light bouncing off of the surface of the pond. A jay shrieked and swooped by. Grinning, Danni began sketching madly. Beneath her quick fingers the pond and its inhabitants materialized. Plump bullfrogs and boxy turtles lined the far bank, calling encouragement to the canoeists. Spotting a watersnake darting away from Tanya's paddle, Danni sketched it in. She chuckled as she added herself poised to fall off of the dock into the water and Mari giving her a final push.

She set her sketch pad down where Mari could see it, and stared out across the water. Mari glanced at the sketch pad indifferently, then froze, her attention caught. "I don't want to be in your picture," she said finally, her voice rusty from disuse.

Danni shrugged and continued to watch the girls splashing and screaming.

"I don't like you," Mari warned, her voice rising. "Don't think that you can get me to like you because you hang out with me and draw. Drawing's lame."

Again Danni shrugged and picked up her sketch pad. Shielding her eyes against the sun's light, she looked toward the line of mountains that fringed the far end of the meadow. At the base of one mountain a line of horses and riders slowly made their way toward the pond. A cloud of dust rose about them, and in the dappled light made them appear as if they were part of a dream.

Danni settled back and began drawing the horses and their small riders with sure, quick lines. Mari was far away from her thoughts.

"Time for our next class," Christine sang out as she pulled her canoe up to the dock. Danni rushed to help the girls unfasten life jackets and stow paddles in their proper places.

"Let's go make ceramics!" Tanya yelled, trying hard to steer her canoe into the dock.

"No, we're supposed to go to the nature center," Jenny reminded her. "Ceramics are after lunch."

"Where's my sketch pad?" Danni asked out loud, looking around.

"Didn't you just bring it down here?" Jenny questioned, looking worried.

"Here it is," Christine called, walking back toward them with a frown. She handed the dusty pad to Danni, who quietly noted that her horse sketch was gone.

"I think Mari helped herself to some of your paper," Christine apologized. "I tried to ask her if she'd seen

40

anything, but she's acting like she's deaf. I just don't know what I should do with her."

"Don't worry about it. Here, I made this for your cabin anyway."

"Danni, you are so sweet. This is *cute!* Hey guys, look at this!" Grabbing Danni in a quick hug, Christine jogged back to her charges. Seconds later Danni could hear the sighted campers explaining to the unsighted ones, "There are turtles, and Tanya's almost running over this skinny green snake that looks totally freaked, and . . ."

At the arts and crafts building David asked Danni to assist the children as they worked on their ceramic mugs. Using small ceramic tools, the girls smoothed the greenware.

"What's greenware?" a blind girl named Lucrecia asked. "Is it green?"

"Not really," David answered. "That's just the name for ceramic before it's fired, or baked."

"Do we get to paint it?" Tanya wanted to know.

"Sure, but first things first—you've got to clean it and sand off all of the rough edges, OK?"

Tanya and Lucrecia groaned good-naturedly and continued to work.

The phone in the storage room shrilled its double ring, and David scooted off to answer it. When he came back he said to Danni, "Eva wants to know if you'd like to help her do some cafeteria decorating. It seems that we have a birthday today."

"Great," Danni said, dusting off her hands and getting up from the table. "I'd love to help."

"If you'll wait just a moment, I'm going down too," Mrs. Ahrens said from the back of the room. She untied her apron and hung it up, then started for the door.

David flashed them both a smile as Jenny's cabin members called goodbye to them.

"What a sweet bunsch of kids," Mrs. Ahrens commented. "They are such fun to work with."

"Yeah, I've really had fun today with all of them, especially Tanya." Danni smiled.

"Have you seen Mari today?" Mrs. Ahrens asked.

Danni nodded.

"She really ticked me off," Danni concluded as she related her experience, "but I guess now we know that she does like horses."

"She fell off a horse when she was 9, and broke several bones in her legs and back. The horse dragged her for a ways before her foot slipped out of the stirrup. As I understand it, she's lucky to be alive."

"She doesn't seem to feel lucky," Danni said.

"No, she doesn't," Mrs. Ahrens mused. "I wonder why."

"Maybe she thinks that it's better to not be here at all than to not be able to do the things that others like to do."

The woman sighed. "Maybe, but that's an awfully sad way to look at things."

Danni shrugged, and they talked of other things.

CHAPTER 5

The Quiet Hour

June 18, Wednesday

Hi, Betti and Dad:

Why did Bart get a dolphin tattoo? Because his girlfriend Autumn did it? Oh, my dumb brother! Please don't let him wear a muscle T-shirt at Fourth of July, please?

Well, this has been a really fun "disABILITY" week, but a lot of work. In a way, it's been good that everybody kind of slows down a bit—walking takes a little while if you can't see or are in a wheelchair. Everybody talks a lot, and we all have stories to tell. It's fun.

A girl named Christine put up on her cabin door a sketch that I drew for her. I feel sorry for her because she's got one of the meanest campers in the whole camp. Mari is only 14, but I feel as if she's a lot older because she cuts me down a lot. She also stole a drawing from me, but I guess that's OK. Is this making sense? What I'm trying to say is that Mari is a camper with problems and she's really hostile and stuff, but all of us are making a real effort to be positive to her and nice to her no matter what. I have to pray a lot to be nice to her. She makes that hard, but . . .

Thanks for the cookies, Daddy. It doesn't matter that

*they were weird shapes, they tasted really good. I am so
sleepy that I . . .*

At the rodeo the band played energetically, and
horses cavorted in the ring. From the back of the yellow
camp truck Danni handed out squirt guns and fake
noses to the last of the clowns and tied her yellow bandanna around her neck more securely.

"Yee-haw!" Gloria whooped, taking her medical kit
out of the truck cab. "Don't I just hate a rodeo."

"You do not," Eva protested with a laugh. "You always say that you can hardly wait for the next one."

"To be over," the other girl retorted. "These things drive
me crazy. Horses were not intended to carry riders waving
banners or running in patterns. Nor were horses meant
to run relays." She closed her medical kit with a bang.

"What were horses intended to do, then?" Eva teased.
Gloria ignored her.

"What's the matter, Glory?" Danni asked. "You really
don't like rodeos?"

"People get hurt," she said tersely.

"Oh," Danni replied, glancing worriedly into the cor-
ral ring.

"It's all right," Eva consoled her, "I'm not really very
fond of these either. Most of the time nothing happens,
but every once in a while someone bumps someone else
or something . . . nothing serious, but . . ."

"I thought girls were supposed to like horses," Jim
Hodges, one of the cowboys, looped his lanky arm
around Gloria and blew in her ear.

"We do like horses," she responded, squirming out of
his grasp and lightly boxing his ears, "but we generally
like riders better—in one piece. Seriously, Jimmy-J, you
guys be careful tonight, you hear? No new routines or
anything, right?"

Jim straightened. "We do have one new routine, when we bring in the flags. We're just going to make a crisscross, circle the ring, and cross back. It's relatively simple."

"OK," Gloria sighed, "and you know where the medical van is parked?"

"Yes, Mother," Jim teased her. "Glo, don't worry so much! It'll be fine." He blew kisses to the three of them and vaulted back into the arena.

Finally, all of the campers had taken seats around the arena and Mr. Ahrens' booming voice invited everyone to stand for prayer and the national anthem. Gloria stood stone-faced as the band played and the riders raced into the arena carrying flags and banners. The flags snapped and rippled as the riders careened around the arena.

As the anthem neared its end, the riders picked up speed and prepared for the crisscross. Danni found that she was holding her breath. Sighing, she consciously released her grip on her felt hat. "Take it easy," she told herself.

The crisscross was flawless. Danni applauded until her palms stung. As Mr. Ahrens announced the names of the riders, Jim trotted by and doffed his hat to Gloria. She rolled her eyes and ignored him.

"Well, the worst is over, thank God," Gloria sighed and settled in to enjoy the rodeo.

Danni especially liked the clowns, as most of their makeup was her creation. Lena from the kitchen and Darla from the pool had volunteered to be clowns, and Danni had gotten a kick out of giving slender Lena a huge pillow belly and long shoes, and Darla's straight locks now hid beneath a wild pink curly wig.

"Uh-oh," Eva chuckled, watching them play leapfrog over each other, "they are going to be filthy—and it looks like we're going to have to patch up Darla's suit."

"Eeeeewwwwww." Danni squinched up her nose. "I wondered why they wore gloves."

"Well, now ya know."

Mr. Ahrens continued to announce each event in carnival fashion, complete with bad jokes and puns. "Now the event all of you have been waiting for, the barrel race!" he bellowed jovially.

"Doesn't he ever run out of voice?" Gloria complained, covering her ears.

"Nope," Eva said.

Danni glanced around the ring at the campers. Although she didn't know many of the male campers, she had met a few of them at the pool and in the cafeteria and waved to a few of them. Kevin, who assisted with a cabin, caught her eye and nodded to her. Across from Kevin sat Christine and Julie's cabin members. Danni was surprised to see Mari sitting up straight and staring at the riders with intense concentration. She pointed this out to Eva, and commented, "I guess she was a pretty serious rider at one time. Mrs. Ahrens told me."

"That would explain why she looks so critically at each rider," Eva nodded. "She probably used to do something like this. Poor girl."

Mr. Ahrens announced the final event—a timed relay of some sort. Danni stretched and prepared to get up and throw away her popcorn bag, when she noticed Gloria's stillness. She sat again and watched.

A rider burst into the arena at high speed. Danni watched as the girl rounded the arena once, twice, then passed off a baton to another rider waiting near the entrance. Mr. A called the girl's time as she left the arena. "34.2 seconds," Danni breathed in awe.

"Not as fast as they get," Eva responded. "Just watch."

The next rider was a young man. He entered the arena at a thundering gallop and flew around the arena. Danni winced at the "*smack!*" she heard as the baton slapped into the palm of the next rider. It must have hurt, because he dropped the baton. A groan went up from the stands.

Instantly, someone produced another baton, and the race went on, but the team was penalized. "39.4 seconds, with a five-second penalty," Mr. Ahrens' sonorous voice boomed.

"Ouch, that really hurt them," Eva remarked. "There's almost no way to make up that time."

The third rider flew into the arena. As he rounded the end of a turn, Danni recognized Jim and focused her attention on him. An excellent rider, he moved gracefully with his horse. "He's fast," she commented.

"Too fast," Gloria breathed.

It all seemed to happen in slow motion. As he rounded the last curve, his hat flew off. Spooked, his horse reared and twisted. Jim hung on grimly, but was dislodged at the last moment by the horse hopping sideways. Frightened by the rider attached to his saddle by only a stirrup, the panicked horse took off toward the open meadow. Danni let out a gasp. Gloria was a blur of motion and was already halfway across the arena toward the other side with her medical kit. Eva grabbed her set of keys and raced toward the medical van, bellowing for someone to stop the horse.

Danni sat down, shaking. Her stomach rolled as she thought about what she had just seen. She was sure that when Jim's head had hit the ground, it had knocked him out cold. Gulping, she looked around wildly.

Mr. Ahrens announced from the bandstand, "Everything's all right, folks. It looks like one of our riders has had a little mishap, but I'm sure that everything is just fine. Right now I'm going to turn the microphone over to my wife, Margery, and she will announce the next rider in this our final event." Mr. Ahrens jogged toward the medical van to ride with Eva.

The baton relay continued, although the riders seemed much more content with slower speeds. The rodeo dragged to an end, and the campers climbed down from their seats around the arena and slowly made their way toward the buses that would take them to their cabins.

The band members collected their instruments, and Danni found herself a part of their group, packing folding chairs into the back of a pickup, picking up trash, and collecting clown equipment.

"You wanna ride back?" one of the band members asked.

"Sure," Danni said listlessly, climbing into the back of their van.

There was still no sign of Eva or Gloria when she arrived at the program room. The clowns had gotten there before her, and were shucking their filthy costumes and wiping paint from their faces. Danni put the makeup away in the cabinet and cleaned the paint from the counters. As she loaded the costumes into the washer she heard a commotion in the upstairs office.

Danni ran upstairs, then slowed. "Don't get in the way," she reminded herself, and continued at a walk.

"Oh, Danni," Lee Macomber said breathlessly, nearly running over her as she came up the stairs, "I was looking for someone—I'm glad I found you. Can you please go and sit with Cabin 12 for about a half hour or so, just until everything calms down? Julie's there, but with disabled campers, it's best to have two in the cabin, just to help out."

"OK, Lee, I'll go right now." Danni scurried out the door.

When she arrived at Cabin 12, she found it in a state of chaos. Julie looked up gratefully as she entered. "Just pitch in anywhere," she said, waving a hand at the mess.

A young girl sat sniffling on the bed. Another one, half in pajamas, and half out, was trying to brush her hair and finish undressing at the same time. A third girl wandered around the cabin, singing softly to herself, as she tried to find her bunk. Julie guided her along and came to stand next to Danni.

"I'll let you in on what happened as soon as we get this lot bedded," she whispered, then in a louder voice, "OK, girls, Danni's filling in until Christine gets back. We need to continue to get ready for bed. Lights off in 10 minutes!"

A chorus of groans and protests filled the cabin. Danni was surprised, though, at how quickly the girls responded. After a snarl in the toothbrushing/last drink line, Danni decided to dispense glasses of water to girls who were sitting on their beds to make things move faster. After brushing one girl's hair and helping another find where she'd put her glasses, most of the girls were quiet and lying down.

"Good job, girls," Julie applauded them. "You have a minute to spare."

"Is Mari OK?" a small voice asked from a bottom bunk. "She can see, so you can't turn out the lights until she gets back."

"She'll be OK, Lu," Julie replied kindly. "When she comes back, Christine will be with her, and she'll have a flashlight, so it'll be OK."

"Why was she crying so loud?" Alice asked, a note of worry in her voice as she fiddled with her glasses.

Julie looked helplessly at Danni. "She was just really upset. She's really OK."

"Can we pray for her?" the girl named Lucrecia asked.

"And for Cowboy Jim," Alice added.

Danni felt her throat getting tight. She looked down

at the floor, blinking rapidly.

"That's a good idea, girls," Julie said. "Danni, will you join us?" Danni nodded and closed her eyes.

"Dear Jesus," Alice started, "we have a request. Mari is our cabinmate, and she's very sad. Can You help her, please? And Jim is hurt . . ." her voice trailed off in a sniffle.

"And so, Father, we ask that You do whatever needs to be done for both of them, if it's Your will. Thank You for being with us. Amen." Julie bent and hugged Alice.

Just then the door opened, and a frazzled-looking Christine entered the cabin. Julie shushed the girls, and Christine announced that Mari had fallen asleep and would stay in the infirmary that night. "She's just fine, and we all need to get to sleep now. Say goodnight to Danni."

"Goodnight!" the girls chorused.

Christine and Julie walked with Danni out to the porch. "What happened?" Danni finally asked.

"She just freaked," Christine said wearily. "Went into hysterics after Jim fell off his horse. At first she started crying softly, then she just kept going and going and pretty soon she was screaming, and I couldn't get her to stop. I was glad Macomber was there to help me with her. The nurse gave her something, and she's out cold."

"Wow," said Danni slowly. "Well, hang in there, girls, we're all praying for you, and the week's almost over."

"Oh, Danni, thanks. You've been a peach." Christine hugged her.

"Jim is better this morning," Mrs. Ahrens announced at morning worship, "but will remain in the hospital under observation for his concussion and broken arm and collar bones for another day. A card is at the front desk in the lodge office for anyone who wants to sign. If anyone needs Gloria, she'll be up and around after breakfast for her regular office hours, but she'll be taking it easy today."

"As for Mari Burtz," Lee Macomber continued, her voice subdued, "she'll be going home today. Her parents are taking a shuttle from the airport to pick her up. Apparently, this is not the first time she has suffered some sort of nervous breakdown since her accident, but this time her parents hope that it is the breakthrough she needed."

Silence. Danni felt her throat tightening and quickly glanced around at the other staff members. *Poor Mari,* she thought. Even after all of the problems she'd given everyone, Danni still felt bad that the girl was going home without making even one friend. On the spur of the moment she stood.

"I—" she cleared her throat and tried again. "I feel like we should maybe make a card for Mari too." Macomber looked interested, and several of the counseling staff nodded, so she continued. "Mari really likes horses, so if some people from Horsemanship would write her a little note, that would make her feel good. Maybe Bill and Glenda from the nature center could say something to her, too. It just doesn't seem right that she should be going home when she was just starting not to be such a grouch. I just feel so bad—" She broke off and shook her head.

"We all do," Macomber assured her, "but we did our best with her, don't you agree?"

Danni nodded miserably.

"Sometimes—and we all need to be reminded of this—we don't get to see the results of the time we spend with our campers. We plant a seed, and the Lord takes care of the watering." Lee Macomber looked seriously at each of the assembled staff members.

"That is why we encourage you to do your best to

share the love of God with each individual camper. You never know what problems they might have, or what kinds of homes they come from, and what you could be doing for them without even knowing it." She turned to Danni. "Why don't you use that fabulous drawing talent I hear you have and design a card for Mari this morning? Then you can take it around before lunch and get everyone to sign it. Will that work out for you?"

Danni nodded. Mrs. Ahrens then made a few more general announcements, and the group dismissed.

Danni hurried out of the side door of the Lupine lodge and down the steps to the ground level. The smell of breakfast cooking floated by as she passed the cafeteria, but she continued climbing down to the meadow floor.

There Danni stood watching the horses graze at the hitching post just beyond the flagpole. She let her imagination take her through dew-misted grasses to the tree line beyond. The sun glinted off the pond. Filled with sudden inspiration, she trotted toward the program room.

By breakfast time Danni had sketched a line of horses wending their way down one of the trails toward the pond. Although she knew that the drawing wasn't exactly like the first one she had done, it was pretty close. Selecting a fine pointed pen from her box, in curling blue letters wrote "Goodbye" at the bottom of the card, then squinted at it critically, not knowing what else to add. Finally she decided to sign her name to the picture, and wrote in tiny letters, "Love, Danni."

The morning dragged for her. After Camp Council she took the short hike up to the nature center. Inside the cool building, as she waited for Glenda to locate Bill, she felt the center's peacefulness begin to calm her. She took a moment to wander through the collection room, admiring the seashells, rocks, insects, and taxidermy models.

"There's more in through here," Glenda called to

her. "Come through the lab here, and look at some of the live animals."

Following her, Danni stepped through the open doorway of the lab, then along a hallway lined with tanks. They contained tarantulas, lizards, frogs, snakes, mice, and other meadow residents. Danni started as she noticed a huge lump in one of the snakes.

"Old Monty the python." Glenda touched his tank affectionately. "I just fed him this morning."

Danni made a horrified face, then burst out laughing. "Guess everything has to eat."

"This is a beautiful card," Bill exclaimed as they met him at the aviary. The chirping of the colorful finches nearly drowned him out. "Make sure that Mr. Ahrens gets to sign it. You just might get yourself a job doing some artwork for the camp."

Danni felt the familiar bubble of excitement begin to work its way through her. Another job! She fairly floated down the hill toward the camp, her heavy mood dissolving. It would be good to get going on something new.

After lunch, Mr. and Mrs. Ahrens, Lee Macomber, and Christine and Julie waited at the Lupine headquarters building for Mari's parents. Danni, passing by to pick up her mail, caught a glimpse of the Burtzes' careworn faces as they spoke with Mr. Ahrens. Gloria assisted Mari to her parents' car and buckled her in. Danni noticed that Gloria had replaced her usually brightly colored clothes with neat white slacks and white coat, and that she had pulled her curly hair back into a professional-looking chignon. Danni could hardly keep from staring.

"Thank you for everything," Mr. Burtz was saying quietly. "We know that you did the best that you knew how."

"Wilbur, we'd better get going, or we'll miss our

flight." Mrs. Burtz tugged gently at her husband's arm.

The couple climbed into the car. As they turned and drove away, Danni saw Mari staring at her. Their eyes locked until the car turned a corner and sped out of sight.

CHAPTER 6

Family

June 28 . . . Friday

Dear Daddy (and Bart):

Brownie camp is almost over, and it'll be July 4 before we know it! I really, really, reeeeeallly hope that you're still coming. I have so much to show you.

I finally got to throw my first pot on my last day off. David helped me during Quiet Hour. He says he never goes to sleep then anyway. I did some swimming too. Lorrie Ann works at the pool. Lorrie Ann is Kevin and Roseanne's cousin, and she's really nice.

I hope that Bart had a nice birthday. Did he get my card? I thought about sending him something for that stupid car of his, but decided a gift certificate would be nicer. He's probably getting fuzzy dice.

I've been getting to sit with cabins during Quiet Hour and during campfires sometimes, but pretty soon it'll be teen camp, and Eva said that since I'm so close to the age of some of the campers I need to be more behind the scenes. I'm working on a mime called "Heartlines" that's about how God heals our hearts. It's pretty funny in some spots, and we're setting it to music. Lena's in it too.

I might get to design the logo for the new camp T-shirts for next summer. Mr. Ahrens already has one of my drawings he wants for a camp postcard. Neat, huh?

Well, that's all for now. Tell Autumn and Betti hello for me, and don't forget to water my cactus every once in a while.

Thanks!

Love ya,

Danni

"So your folks are coming up for Family Camp?" Kevin asked as they walked toward the cabin area.

"Yeah—aren't your mom and dad coming up too?"

"Only for a day." Kevin raked his fingers through his mop of strawberry blond hair and readjusted his cap. "With all of my little foster brothers and sisters, it would be too hard for Mom and Dad to stay any longer."

"They must really miss your help."

"Actually, Ursula's 12 and Kym is 9. They help out a lot."

"That's good." Danni smiled politely.

"Hey, Danni," Glenda called, jogging over, "have you seen Bill anywhere?"

"No, we just finished cleaning cabins on the first row, and we're looking for Macomber. What's up?"

"I need some serious help at the nature center. It's one of the biggest attractions of Family Camp, and it looks like a tornado just went through there. The sawdust for the bottom of the rodent cages is covering everything, the rock collections are all over everywhere, and some of the lizards are missing."

"Who would have done that?" Kevin blurted.

Glenda smiled at his horrified expression. "The problem is, I think I know who did it—Gaddabout. But I can't find him anywhere."

"Gaddabout?" Danni asked curiously.

"Her raccoon," Kevin grinned. "He's cute."

"But he's also a menace to society." Glenda frowned. "He always does this kind of stuff when I don't have time to deal with it. If I find Macomber and clear it with her, you guys want to help me out?"

"Sure," Kevin and Danni responded in unison, then laughed at how they had answered simultaneously.

"You two have been working together too long," Glenda chuckled, then went off in search of Lee.

Two hours later Danni unplugged the vacuum cleaner and dusted off her hands with a sigh. "The havoc one raccoon can wreak." She shook her head.

"I know, can you believe this?" Kevin finished wiping out a drinking fountain. "And the worst thing is, he left his paw prints *everywhere*."

"We just have the downstairs display cases to work on and the glass doors out front, and then we're through," Glenda announced, coming out of the lab. "I took all of the rocks out of the water wheel fountain, and put them back on the display tables. Wonder how he got out?"

"Better check his cage," Danni rubbed her neck. "You don't want to go through this again."

"Hear, hear," Kevin said.

"I just wish I knew if he was ready to go back to the wild," Glenda said. "When I picked him up, he was so small, and his foot had been crushed by a car or something." She sprayed window cleaner on a glass display case, while Danni and Kevin started on the doors.

"It's not as if I'm not willing to let a wild creature go back to the wild, it's just—well, he was my baby," she continued, wiping vigorously. "I guess now I'm ready to realize that he needs to be outside."

"Well, that's a good thing," Bill commented as he bounded down the stairs. "It looks like Gadz has been outside and has already got a good start on making friends. I saw a second set of paw prints outside of the telescope tower."

"How do you know it's Gaddabout?" Danni wondered.

"Having a crushed foot gives one some pretty distinctive paw prints," the blond-haired naturalist explained. "Just to make sure, I'll watch for him tonight and get a good look at him. Kevin, care to stay up at the telescope tower with me tonight?"

"Definitely." Kevin gave his usual one-word response.

Glenda caught a glimpse of Danni's expression. "Danni, I guess we'll do it another time." She smiled. "Don't worry! We've got all summer, and the stars will still be there."

"I guess," Danni agreed reluctantly.

"Well, let's finish up. It's going on 4:00." Bill grabbed a paper towel and began to vigorously rub down some of the display cases.

"Four o'clock? My folks will be here in half an hour!" Danni scrambled to put the vacuum cleaner away.

Her parents met her at the Lupine Meadow Lodge where they had chosen to stay instead of in a cabin. Danni was surprised to see her brother's girlfriend, Autumn, with them. "Are you here for the whole week?" she asked her politely.

"No," Autumn responded breezily, flinging back a hank of her long black hair with beringed fingers. "We've got too much work to do," she continued with a significant glance at Bart. He straightened self-consciously and ran a nervous hand through his dark crew cut.

"Uh, yeah, Danni, we're getting married at the end of the summer." He waited for her response.

Danni blinked. *After going with her only three months?* Taking her cue from the polite smiles her father and step-mother, Betti, gave her, Danni said cautiously, "Well, this *is* a surprise. Congratulations! Do you have a date set?"

"Well, not quite." Bart gave his father a sideways glance. "We're still working out some details."

"You're welcome to come, of course," Autumn invited her.

Danni stared. "I *hope* I'm invited," she replied, giving Bart a hard look.

"Well, we're going for a nontraditional approach," Danni's brother explained hastily, "and we're only going to be a few friends getting together on a beach."

"Oh," Danni said slowly, "I see. So, are you staying for this whole week?"

"As a matter of fact, he is," Daddy cut in briskly, and Bart looked startled, "so I suggest, Autumn, that you should start on your way. It's a far piece to drive, and you'll want to get home before it gets too late."

"Sure, Mr. Mallory," Autumn chirped. "C'mon Bartles, walk me to my car." Bart gave his father an angry look, and trailed out the door after his fiancée.

Danni stood looking at the door long after they had gone. Her father shifted uncomfortably behind her. Finally she spoke, not turning. "Well?"

"Well, I just found out a few minutes ago myself, girl," her father said mildly.

"And you're going to let him do this? He would marry the first fool who came along." Her voice was thick with tears.

"Now Danni-Dee," her father's voice was gentle, "Autumn's not so bad. We've always known that Bart will always march to his own drumbeat."

"We've also always known," Betti's voice was soft, "that the Lord will walk with him, as long as he allows Him to."

"I know." Danni turned reluctantly to her parents. "It's just hard to watch him be someone else besides just my brother. I've hardly gotten to know him now that we're older, and now he's off to marry someone. And why did they have to announce it this week? I've been looking forward to you guys coming forever, but he's spoiled it."

"Nothing is spoiled, Danni," Betti smiled at her. "We'll all spend this time alone together this week, and maybe Bart will come to some new opinions about people, or maybe he won't. Either way, it'll be family time, and Bart knows that, even though he didn't come prepared to spend a week."

"What's he going to wear, then?" asked Danni, confused.

"Oh, I brought him clothes," Betti grinned.

Danni laughed out loud at the woman who had been her mother since she was 9 years old. "Thanks, Betti. I'm sure he'll appreciate it when he gets over being mad." They both laughed. Then Danni said seriously, "I just hope that he knows what he's doing."

Her father put a hand on her shoulder. "Just keep him in your prayers," he reminded her.

"Another day, another bathroom," Kevin quipped, meeting Danni at the RV area after worship.

"Yuck, and before breakfast, too," she groaned. "This will give me a new appreciation for all the work my mom did when we were kids."

"And then some," Kevin added.

"Do you want to start on the guy's side or what?" she asked, picking up the "Wet Floor" sign.

"Why don't we start with the laundromat first? At this time of day, nobody's started washing clothes yet, but there's bound to be someone still in the shower."

Shuddering at the thought, Danni followed Kevin to

the laundromat. After they had wiped out machines and cleaned out the dryer filters, Kevin broke the silence. "I saw your brother yesterday at the pool. He and Lorrie Ann seem to have really hit it off. Did they know each other before, or what?"

Danni made a disgusted noise. "No, my brother is just the biggest known flirt in the Western world. I hope Lorrie Ann drops him flat. He's supposed to be engaged."

"Oh, really?" Kevin turned to her. "Anyone Rose-anne and I would know?"

"No," Danni hedged, "she doesn't come to church much. Bart met her at the Boardwalk at the end of last school year."

"Oh, well that's nice. Have they set a date?"

"I hope they never do," she muttered under her breath.

After again saying "Oh," Kevin turned back to his work.

Danni sighed. "I just found out yesterday, and I feel . . . funny about it."

Kevin paused, then asked, "Have you talked to him?"

"No . . . I don't want to give him the third degree," she began.

"Does it have to be an interrogation? You're his sister. If you tell him you're worried about him, at least he'll know you care. Now if I was getting ready to do something Rosey or Ursula thought was stupid, they'd sure tell me."

Danni smiled at the thought of Roseanne giving Kevin an earful. "Well, if you don't think it's none of my business . . ."

"He'll let you know if he doesn't like it," Kevin shrugged.

They worked their way through both bathrooms. The camp was waking up, and it was almost time for breakfast. As Danni hauled a scrub bucket of dirty water out of the last bathroom, two girls careened around the corner, nearly colliding with her. She slung the bucket out of the way to avoid hitting them. Unfortunately, at that moment, a heavyset woman walked around the corner, and the water only narrowly avoided splashing directly in her face.

"Oh," Danni gasped, "I'm sorry, I'm so sorry." With shaking hands she set the bucket down and surveyed the damage. "I didn't get your shoes wet, did I?"

The woman glowered at her. "Whatever possessed you to dump the water from that doorway? Kids these days," she snarled, stomping through the puddle into the bathroom. Kevin, who was watching, grinned at her.

"Close call," he commented dryly.

"Oh, is it only 8:00 a.m?" she moaned as they trudged off to clean up the mess.

Bart dove cleanly into the deep end of the pool. Danni, from her perch at the foot of Lorrie Ann's lifeguard chair, applauded him.

"Thank you, thank you," he bowed gracefully to her and slicked back his hair. "Why don't you get back in, Danni?"

"Why don't you get out, Bart? Aren't you hungry yet?"

"Nope. Didn't get up until late, and had a late breakfast. I'll keep you company, though." He pulled his lanky frame out of the pool. His tattoo glistened wetly.

"Your tattoo finally looks happy," Danni teased him as he waved goodbye to Lorrie Ann.

"Yeah, Flipper got his fill of water."

"It doesn't look as bad as I thought it would. Didn't it hurt?"

"A bit."

"What happens when you want to get it taken off?"

"Who says I want it taken off?" Bart turned to her.

"Well, who's ever heard of a neurosurgeon with a dolphin tattoo?" Danni returned.

"Lighten up, Danni, it'll be in memory of my trip over fool's hill. Why don't you try going over it sometime? It might do you some good." He dodged her swipe at his arm and changed the subject.

"Does that Lorrie Ann have anyone she's seeing up here?"

"No, but you don't care, Bart. Remember you're engaged."

"Oh." Bart wrinkled his brow.

They walked in silence for a while. He pulled his tank top on as they approached the cafeteria. "Do you want to sit outside or inside?" Danni asked.

"I'm not going in with a wet behind!" Bart punched her lightly.

"Well, pick a table; I'll be right out. Take in the view—" She waved a hand at the meadow and entered the building.

"So you love it here," he began as she filled her mouth with a bite of salad.

"Bart!" she protested around a mouthful of food.

"OK, sorry, chew," he responded teasingly, waving his hand.

When she had swallowed, she replied, "Yes, I love it here. I've met a lot of really neat people."

"Yeah, that Gloria . . ." Bart shook his head admiringly.

"Hello, hormones. Earth to Bartholomew Mallory, do you read me? You're engaged."

"Would you quit with the engaged stuff?" Bart flared. "It's not like I'm married already or anything. Or that I'm blind. I'm just looking."

"Touchy!"

"I'm serious," he snapped. "Just lay off on me, OK?"

"Well, you're the one who got engaged and wants everyone to take it so seriously. How serious is it if you still flirt like there's no tomorrow?"

"I take Autumn seriously," Bart retorted, "but it's not like all of that, OK? We're just casual in this relationship, you know?"

"Right." Danni rolled her eyes. "Like marriage is casual."

He scowled and looked away.

Danni finished the last bite of her salad and sighed. Their conversation had not turned out like she had planned. "I don't mean to nag you, Bart," she said in a softer voice. "I just can't believe the whole thing, you know?"

He shrugged and looked away from her out into the meadow. Horses stood by the hitching post, swishing their long tails at the flies. Danni breathed in the peacefulness of the scene . . . then she checked her watch and groaned.

"I've got to go back to work," she sighed. "I can't believe that a whole hour just went by. Shall I meet you for dinner, or are you still cranky?"

He glared at her, then gave a reluctant grimace. "OK. Dinner."

"See you then," she said, then went off waving and blowing kisses. He stuck out his tongue.

After they finished the bathrooms in the crafts building, Kevin and Danni took a breather to visit with David.

"I'll bet you never knew how many bathrooms there were at this camp," David laughed.

"I sure didn't," Kevin said.

"We've figured out a way to save the best two for last, though," Danni told the older boy.

"The *best* two?" David raised his eyebrows.

"Yeah," Kevin said. "The nature center has great air-conditioning and four bathrooms in the same building. And the pool—well, I've got my suit and Danni has hers and Lorrie Ann promised that the pool would close half an hour before dinner so that everybody would be out of there."

"Membership has some definite privileges," David laughed with them.

"Well, I hope you have a great week." Danni waved to him as they started down the trail.

"Same to you," he called.

"He sure is a nice guy," Danni remarked.

"Yeah, Bill says he's been here three summers and the Ahrenses don't know what they'd do without him. He's done almost everything around here, including help out at Cowboy."

"Really?" Danni was surprised. "I didn't know he rode horses."

"Wait 'til the next rodeo," Kevin assured her. "You'll see."

Campfire was over, and most of the log benches were deserted. A knot of chilly campers crowded in close to the fire, roasting marshmallows and chatting idly. Bart and Danni, zipped up into heavy down jackets, sat with their feet pointed toward the blaze, leaning on a pile of logs. Danni looked hesitantly at Bart, then, with a quick prayer for the right words, leaned toward her brother. "Bart?" she said softly.

"What?" he said, his voice low.

"Are you really engaged?"

"Yes, Danni, I'm 'really engaged,'" Bart replied in an aggravated voice. "I thought we had dropped this one."

She waited a moment, then ventured another question. "Are you happy about it?"

Bart sighed, then sat quietly for a moment, studying his fingernails, his tanned face serious. "No," he said, finally, "but it's too late for that. She's already told her parents."

"What?" Danni exclaimed. "I thought you guys had decided this only today!"

"Well, we've been thinking about it for a while, and I

guess she thought that she had the go-ahead. She's already invited people and figured out what she wants, so . . ." he shrugged. "It means a lot to her, Danni. You know how it is."

His sister was speechless. "But, Bart, really! Just because she wants you to do this doesn't mean that you have to!" She scooted to her knees, hands clasped. "This is your life we're talking about here! You're only 19! Why do you have to do this now?" When he didn't respond, she snapped, "Sometimes you are just too easy going for your own good."

He shrugged.

It took 20 minutes of cajoling, begging, pleading, and bargaining before she could get Bart to even admit that he might be making a mistake. Danni dragged him to the lodge to talk to their parents. They had just reached it when their parents showed up.

"Hey, fancy meeting you here!" Betti said as she unlocked the door.

"We need to talk to you both," Danni said.

"About my wedding . . ." Bart began.

Thursday was officially Danni's day off, but she could hardly stand to think about how much work Eva was doing by herself for the Fourth of July celebration. "I still can't believe you talked me into taking today off," Danni complained. "How do you expect me to just sit back while you do all of this work?" She took another bite of her pancake.

"It's OK," Eva reassured her. "I really have no intention of doing more than I have to. There's the rodeo tonight, there will be fireworks afterward, and those are the main activities for today. I have lots of help."

"Well, let me know if you need me to do anything for you, OK?"

Eva laughed. "Danni, the filthy clown outfits will be waiting in a bag tomorrow just for you. Relax!"

Just then the woman Danni had nearly splashed with mop water entered the cafeteria. Her eyes met Danni's, and she looked offended. "Good morning," the girl ventured timidly. The woman stalked off with a sniff.

"That's Mrs. Vietz. What did you ever do to her?" Eva looked surprised.

When Danni quickly recounted the story, the older girl burst into giggles. "Cheer up," she chortled, "it could have been worse. She could have actually been coming *out* of the shower instead of going in!"

Danni grimaced. "Hey," she said, changing the subject, "is David riding in the rodeo tonight? That's what I had heard."

Caught off balance, Eva stuttered, "What?" Recovering herself she said, "Not that I know of. Where did you hear that?"

Danni frowned. "Maybe it was supposed to be a surprise. Kevin said he was working with them."

"Oh, really," Eva said, feigning disinterest. "Well, I guess he can if he wants to. The cowboy staff do their own thing; I just help out for the evening."

"Oh." Danni felt compelled to drop the subject. "Well," she said lamely, "have a good day."

"I will," Eva said, sounding distracted as she walked into the kitchen.

Danni spent the morning at the arts and crafts building with her stepmother, painting a porcelain plate. Betti's roses looked plump and red next to Danni's slim pink buds. "Art is imitating life here," Betti said wryly. "Danni, how do you make your flowers look like that?"

The girl shrugged. "I don't know how I do it; this is

just the way it turns out. I like yours and you like mine. Wanna trade?"

"No, I'm sending mine to my mother. She'll never believe that I did this, so I have to have proof. What are you going to do with yours?"

"Guess," Danni teased.

"Oh, so I get it anyway," Betti laughed.

"I wonder how the great archers are doing," Danni commented. Bart and her father were out on the archery range for their third competition.

"I don't know, but it's getting rather warm in here." Betti frowned. "Do you want to go to the pool? It's where Bart will likely show up after he beats your father."

"Yeah, let's go," Danni bounced up. "I hardly ever get to swim, and you really should meet Lorrie Ann."

"A lifeguard?" Betti wanted to know.

"Yep. And Bart's newest obsession."

"Not again!" the woman groaned.

Supper was a Western affair with chili dogs and watermelon. Danni looked over the huge crowd of campers and tried to find her parents.

"Danni! Danni!" Eva elbowed her way frantically through the crowd. The girl started toward her. "What's the matter, Eva?"

She sighed in exasperation. "Katherine Armstrong was all set to sing the national anthem for the rodeo, then she just backed out on me. I needed two more clowns, and Lorrie Ann volunteered to fill one spot, so I still have to find one more. I'm sorry to dump this on you on your day off—"

"Say no more!" Danni giggled, suddenly struck by an idea. "I know someone who would make a great clown!"

Eva looked tense. "There's one more thing. It would

be a huge favor to me—would you sing the national anthem for me? Please?"

Danni's mouth dropped open. "Eva! The last time I sang in public was when I was in kindergarten. Don't you think someone else would be better?"

Eva shook her head. "Nope. I've heard you sing, kiddo. Will you do it? Your parents will be really proud of you."

"But I don't have time to practice!"

The older girl threw up her hands. "Please don't tell me that you don't know the words!"

Danni laughed nervously. "OK, OK. I—I'll do it. But you owe me one!"

Eva gave her a quick hug. "I know it, hon. Thanks." She raced off. Danni dived into the crowd to locate her brother.

"This stuff is sticky," Bart said for the fourth time, resisting the urge to scratch his nose.

"You get used to it," Lorrie Ann said. The campers had just arrived at the rodeo arena, and Bart was taking a breather from chasing her around with a watergun.

"Well, I'm glad you're doing this with me," Bart replied. "I can't believe my sister roped me into this."

"That's programming for you. Anyone can be the next victim," Danni chuckled.

"Even you," Eva teased her. "Ready?"

"As I'll ever be," Danni sighed, feeling the butterflies in her stomach metamorphize into eagles.

"Smile, it won't be that bad," Gloria reassured her, taking her usual place on the bandstand with her medical kit.

"I'll be right here," Bart said in a low voice. Danni looked down at him gratefully, then grinned. He didn't really look too comforting with the green wig he wore.

"Well, we'd better go," Lorrie Ann touched Bart's arm.

He turned to her with his watergun ready. "Start running," he teased. Danni watched them go with an unsteady smile. She wanted more than anything to be running away with them—anywhere other than where she was.

Mr. Ahrens walked up to the bandstand and rifled through his music. He saw Danni watching him, and gave her a wink. "I hear you're going to favor us with a song," he rumbled. "Do you want the band to play along with you?"

Yes! Drown me out! she thought to herself. "No, thank you," Danni said uncomfortably. "I'm going to do it a capella."

"Very nice. Shall I introduce you?"

"Oh, no, please no," she babbled. "My parents will know who it is."

Mr. Ahrens laughed gently. "OK, Danni, no introduction. If anyone else wants to know who sang, I'll tell them to ask your parents."

Danni blushed crimson, then had to laugh. "You can say who it was afterward."

The camp director nodded.

The campers had taken their seats and Mr. Ahrens gave Danni her cue. She stood before the microphone and looked up. Through the starry sky one lone star stood out brightly. Danni breathed the cool night air and stared up at that beautiful star. She willed the fluttering in her stomach to cease.

"Oh! say, can you see,
     by the dawn's early light,
  What so proudly we hailed
     at the twilight's last gleaming,"

She heard her voice echo across the meadow. The thunder of horses' hooves drowned out the sound, as several cowboys rode into the arena, each carrying a flag. They rode in formation, using the crisscross style that Danni was familiar with. One of the riders was

David, looking handsome and serious in his Western shirt and hat.

"Whose broad stripes and bright stars
 thro' the perilous fight,
O'er the ramparts we watch'd,
 were so gallantly streaming?"

Danni took a deep breath, aware that her legs were shaking. She glanced across the arena and froze. Several military veterans stood arrow straight with hands placed reverently over their hearts. Danni saw her father, a Vietnam veteran, with his eyes closed. Her voice wavered and her throat nearly closed from nerves. Then from far away, she heard a voice singing with her. It was Bart. Taking courage from his voice, she lifted her head and sang.

"And the rocket's red glare,
 the bombs bursting in air,
Gave proof thro' the night
 that our flag was still there."

Other voices joined in. First Mr. Ahrens, singing quietly. Then members of the band. Finally, the whole arena picked up the refrain.

"Oh, say does that star-spangled banner yet wave
O'er the land of the free
And the home of the brave."

The echo across the meadow acted as a benediction. Then the applause deafened her. Danni stumbled over to Bart and hugged him tightly, tears rolling down her cheeks. She had paint on her face, but she didn't care.

"Good job, baby sister," her brother said softly. "You did all right."

"It's not much of an encore for a stellar musician like yourself," Kevin teased the following morning as a bleary-eyed Danni joined him to clean the RV area bathrooms, "but you must admit, it *is* a living."

"I stayed up waaay too late," she admitted. "You just don't know what an effort it was getting up this morning. After yesterday, today is sort of a letdown." She sighed dramatically. "And to top it all off, my parents are leaving tomorrow."

"My folks really enjoyed the show last night," Kevin said as he opened a dryer in the laundromat and pulled out a lint-ridden filter.

"They were here *yesterday?*" she squeaked, feeling her face grow warm. "I can't believe that out of all the days during this week they could have picked, they picked yesterday."

"Well, yesterday was the only day this week that was a holiday. Of course, they came up for the Fourth. Anyway," he slammed the dryer shut, "like I was saying, they really enjoyed the show—especially my dad. He thinks you could have a career in singing if you wanted to."

"Really?" For a moment she imagined herself standing in the spotlight with an orchestra behind her. Then she thought of the terrifying moment before she heard her brother singing with her and shuddered at the memory. "No thanks, I'll stick to drawing or something."

They had almost finished the RV area when Mrs. Vietz bustled around the corner. Danni had a sinking feeling when the woman's eyes landed on her. "Good morning," she said.

The woman looked at her sharply. "If you could be as good at having common sense as you are at singing, you might just amount to something," she said in a clipped voice. Danni suddenly felt an inch tall.

"I hope you enjoyed your stay here," Danni muttered, remembering Mr. Ahrens' insistence on politeness to all of the campers.

"If you didn't, I don't think you can blame Danni," Kevin said firmly, and led Danni away. "Just ignore her," he said as they headed toward the cafeteria bathrooms. "I have heard horror stories about her all week. Don't take her griping personally. She must just be an unhappy person."

"I guess it's just an occupational hazard of working at camp," Danni agreed glumly.

"Cheer up, we get to eat breakfast." He poked her. "Food always does the trick for me." He broke into a lazy trot. She looked incredulously after him, then followed suit into the brightly lit building.

July 9 . . . Tuesday

Dear D.D.:

I had a good time hanging out with you, baby sister. It looks like Lupine Meadows is something that's really done you a lot of good. Maybe next summer I'll see if I can get in on their lifeguarding staff or in the infirmary or something. Summer school is kind of boring now in comparison.

I found out a little something that you might like to know. Autumn is pregnant. And no, don't even think it. She was pretty upset when I talked to her about putting off our wedding, and it finally all came out. I don't think the baby's father is interested in the baby at all.

I told Autumn that I would still be her friend, so now I have a nephew or niece in the works. I might even get to be her Lamaze coach—isn't that weird? I'm just glad that I got out of the whole thing before it was too late.

Hey, if you see Lorrie Ann, tell her I got her letter, and will write back as soon as I can. Tell Gloria that I miss her. Tell Glenda that I really enjoyed all the time I spent at the nature center, and . . . well, just tell all the girls I'm glad I met them.

Vaya con Dios, D.

Bart

CHAPTER 7

A Tough Act to Follow

The stage lights were blinding as Danni stepped out from behind the makeshift curtain. She strained to see, but stopped after her efforts made her eyes water. The music started, and she moved slowly to the left part of the stage, trying her best to look confused and forlorn.

Danni felt, more than saw, Lena's graceful form start after her. Recognizing her cue, Danni turned and started motioning her over. Lena responded, and their silent dialogue continued.

As she exited the stage, Danni realized that she was sweating. "Whew!" she exclaimed, "those spotlights are not only blinding, they're broiling too!"

Eva laughed at her. "After you've been doing it for a while, it's not so bad. You looked great."

"Thanks." Danni bowed modestly. "Now what can I do to be your numero uno stagehand?"

"Actually, I don't need too much help until the final scenes—I just need you to remove two chairs from the props while Lena adds a small table and a vase with a rose in it. The lights will be down while you do it, but it shouldn't be a great big deal." Eva paused with her hand on the earpiece of her headset.

"OK, we're about ready to go into the third scene. Be ready in just a few, OK?"

Danni stood tensed and ready to dart out on stage to retrieve the chairs. Next to her, Lena waited with table and vase in hand. The lights dropped, and the music shifted to a soothing murmur.

"OK, now," Eva whispered, and Danni started across the stage. It was much darker than she expected. The fire in the firebowl cast eerie light that flickered in odd patterns. Danni saw the chairs glinting in the light, and grabbed them. On her return trip, however, disaster struck.

Thump, Crash!

The toe of her sandal had gotten pinched between two of the boards that made up the stage floor, and she had tripped and gone flying. Stunned, she groped for her chairs, and tried to scramble up, but her shoe was still stuck. The music was growing louder as a cue for the next actors to come on stage. The lights went back up, and David stepped out on stage.

Danni could feel her ears burning. Her hands shook as she pulled her shoe free. So far, no one in the audience seemed to know that she was not a part of the act. David stepped over to her, and gently pulled her up. She nodded to him, and gracefully departed with her chairs. Just as smoothly, Lena stepped behind them and deposited her table and vase. They both left the stage, and David continued with his miming.

Backstage, Eva said, "Oh, Danni, I'm so sorry! I tried to tell them not to put the lights back up, but with this kind of thing, it's hard to stop without interrupting the flow of the music. Are you OK?"

Danni nodded breathlessly.

"Good. Be ready in a few minutes to go back out and remove the table and vase. You might want to take off your shoes. Now Lena—"

Danni looked at her in amazement. "But—"

"What's wrong?" Eva asked quickly.

"Nothing, but, you want me to go back out there?"

"Yes. Now."

Danni kicked off her sandals and went.

After the campers had gone to bed, some of the staff congratulated Danni on her acting abilities. "Hey, Danni, you really pulled that off well," Kevin said, grinning.

"If I hadn't seen this mime already five times this summer, I would never have known you didn't belong," Lorrie Ann added.

"Really," David agreed. "You were just another one of the people the Christian in the mime was called on to help. It really worked in just fine."

"I thank you all for trying to make me feel better," Danni blushed.

Just then Kat Armstrong came up to the group. "Hey, *Grace,*" she drawled. "Have a nice trip?"

Danni's face burned again. "New legs," she replied lightly and turned away to find Eva.

"Maybe you guys should cast me in one of the skits next time," Kat persisted, following her.

"Sure, if you're interested, talk to Eva." Danni began putting props in boxes to carry to the prop room in the program office.

"Well, I'm talking to you." Kat planted herself in Danni's path. "Eva doesn't like to put regular people in her little plays, so I can't ask her. I'm asking you, and I want to be put in a play with David Taylor."

"What do you mean, 'regular people'?" Danni asked, coming to a halt.

"Don't play stupid. You know how all the minorities hang together." She waved her hands to stall Danni's reply. "Just get me into a decent play," she repeated.

For a moment Danni felt angry and tempted to slap Kat. She took a deep, steadying breath and sent up a quick prayer. Then, seeing the funny side of things, she chuckled.

Startled, Kat stepped back. "What's funny?" she asked suspiciously.

"You are. You'll make a great actor! I'll talk to Eva about you being a character in one of the melodramas on Saturday night. Good night, Kat!" She turned away quickly and started toward the program office.

"So she wants to be in a melodrama with David, does she?" Eva said.

"It's not really funny," Gloria said seriously. "Kat was here last summer, and she still doesn't have a very good attitude. I'm not looking forward to IC Week this year. It won't be a lot of fun."

"What's IC Week?" Danni wanted to know.

"Inner-City Week. We get kids from all over. It's sponsored by the churches in the inner cities—they basically get together all of the kids who are interested, and they come."

"It's mostly Latino and Black kids from low-income areas," Eva added. Turning to her roommate, she asked, "Gloria, do you really feel that Kat is going to be a problem this year?"

Gloria shrugged. "Last year she was at the Mountain Lore base camp helping with the cooking. She told a lot of people that she was glad she didn't have to work with the 'wetbacks.'" Eva winced. "We don't really have a place to send her this year, do we? We're expecting such a big group this time that we'll need all of our staff assistants to run games and supervise activities. What are we going to do?"

"Talk to Macomber, for one thing," Eva said decidedly. "I don't like how Katherine approached Danni."

Danni sighed. "Eva, it wasn't a big deal."

"Danni, maybe it wasn't a big deal to you, but at Lupine Meadows it's important that people learn to work together. You didn't think that we were just here to minister to the kids, did you? We're also here to minister to each other. This just became my special project. I'm going to do something about it."

"Look out, Kat," Gloria muttered under her breath. Eva pinched her on her way out the door.

July 15 . . . Monday

Dear Betti, guess what?

Eva finally heard from her friend Jeannie. She did go off for a while with some teacher of hers, but she found out that he was married, and one of his kids had been in her sociology class or something. Anyway, she's back with her parents now, and Eva and Gloria went to see her. I'm just glad that she's OK. I can't imagine just taking off with someone, but Gloria said she knew another girl who did something like that, only she didn't come back. She lives in Japan now with the Japanese teacher—who is also her husband. But isn't married. Or, he wasn't then. Anyway, you get what I mean.

I just thought I'd tell you because you were still praying for Jeannie.

Thanks, Betts!

P.S. Check out the artwork on the postcard—I could do something like that.

Love you all,

Danni

CHAPTER 8

The Eyes Have It

"I don't think it's fair," Lena was saying hotly as she and Danni and Roseanne walked toward the cafeteria. "I had my day off request slip in long before Suzanne and Kat had theirs in, and they got their first choice. Darla, Lorrie Ann, and I were told that we could have our turn next time. Where does Macomber get off doing that? This is going to be a horrible week. She makes me so mad!" Her dark eyes flashed as she walked rapidly up the stairs.

Usually mild-mannered, Lena's anger surprised Danni. "It sounds like you're fed up about a lot of things," she observed.

"I am! This afternoon only Adrian, Maria, and a few others got to stay and cool off at the pool after Quiet Hour. Darla and I had to go right back to work! And what hurts the most is that we had all been working together! Why does Macomber like them better?"

"She doesn't," Darla said soothingly. "Maybe she had them do something else. Who knows? Don't assume the worst, Lena."

"Well, I don't know," Lena sniffed, "but she'd better stay out of my way for the rest of this week, even if that is only today." She picked up a cafeteria tray and banged it down on the counter.

"I've noticed myself that Macomber isn't like she usually is, if that's any help to you," Darla commented. "I think everybody is just getting that middle-of-the-summer slump."

"It's not even the middle of the summer yet!" Lena protested, giving herself a spoonful of macaroni and cheese with a vigorous "thump."

"I don't know what's wrong," Danni said listlessly. "It's affecting everybody." *Even Eva and Gloria,* she thought.

"Hiya, Brown Eyes," Perry, one of the kitchen supervisors sang out. "Would you like an ice-cream sundae with your lunch today?"

"Sure," Lena said, her bad mood dissolving under his friendly brown gaze. "And you'll take me to Barney's on your next day off?"

"No," Perry laughed, "you can have it today!" And he placed a bowl loaded with vanilla ice cream, chocolate syrup, nuts, and sprinkles on her tray.

Lena's eyes bugged out. "Perry, are you going to get in trouble for this?" she whispered.

"Nope," he grinned, "it's on the house." He smiled at Roseanne. "How about you, Rosie?"

She gave him an odd look. "Sure," she responded cautiously, glancing at Danni.

Danni smiled as she slid her tray across the metal counter. Perry returned her smile a little strangely. "Sorry toots," he waved his hand at her, "we're all out."

Lena gave him a horrified glance. "Perry!"

"Sorry, Brown Eyes," he shrugged, and walked away.

Continuing down the counter, Danni picked up a bowl of fruit salad and a dish of baked apples. Just as she was turning to leave the line, she saw Perry return to the counter. "Hey sport," he greeted the next staff member, "howza 'bout some ice cream to brighten up your day?"

Danni stood nailed to the spot. Darla stared next to

her. Perry flicked a glance at them and continued to pass out ice cream. "I'll give you some of mine," Darla finally said.

"Actually, I'm not that hungry," Danni admitted, turning to find a table.

Later that afternoon Danni walked up to the crafts building to talk to David. She was feeling homesick and tired. "Hi, David," she said, seeing him at his pottery wheel.

"Oh, hi," he said distractedly. "What do you need?"

"Nothing, really," she replied, startled. "I was just coming to see you."

"Well, I'm really busy," he replied in an unusually sharp voice. "Why don't you go and hang out with . . . blondie-what's-her-name—Lorrie Ann at the pool?"

She shrugged. David sounded tired too. "See you later," she mumbled, and started toward the lodge.

The ice-cream incident was on her mind the following morning as they waved goodbye to the campers who were pulling away on their buses toward home. The entire staff turned out every Sunday morning at 7:30 to wave goodbye, and Danni took the opportunity to seek Perry out and talk to him. When she walked toward him, however, he turned away.

"Perry—" she broke off hesitantly.

"What?" He turned around, dark eyes surly.

"I just wanted to . . . to apologize if I've done anything to make you feel badly toward me. I have always thought of you as a friend, and I hope that nothing changes that." She waited.

He stood still for a moment, then ducked his head. "Whatever," he muttered and stalked away.

Danni felt a sadness such as she had never known

before. The whole past week had seemed off-kilter and strange. Even Gloria and Eva had seemed distant. First David and now Perry seemed too occupied to even talk. Waves of loneliness rolled through her. For the first time that summer, she wanted to go home.

Kevin walked across the parking lot with his cap pulled down. His blue eyes were red rimmed, and he looked exhausted as he gave Danni a tired smile.

"OK, folks," Mr. Ahrens rumbled, "let's get staff meeting rolling, shall we?" He waded through the crowd of milling people and entered the lodge. The camp staff followed a little more slowly.

"We have a very important group to get ready for this afternoon," he began after the group settled. "Our inner-city kids have some special needs that we need to be aware of. I'm told that some of you have been preparing for those needs already. Eva Davies, front and center."

"Thanks, Mr. A," Eva said, taking a position at the front of the room. She stood and looked out at the staff, and once again Danni saw how small she was. She appeared to be deciding what to say, and looked hesitant. Danni sought her eyes, and gave her an encouraging smile. Eva smiled back, suddenly standing straighter.

"Thank you, Danni," she said. "I've been wondering how to say this, and Danni has given me the courage to go on. Some of you may have noticed this week that things have been a little strained. A number of you have been feeling angry and hurt, some of you have wanted to go home. I've heard that a lot of you think that the executive staff have treated you unfairly. We have. But there's been a 'method to our madness.'" She smiled sadly.

"This week we have given all of you a little taste of a poison called 'prejudice.' You may have noticed that some people seemed to get a lot of breaks this week. Some had longer free time from work. Some people got to be late to appointments, and received only the slightest discipline. Some people even got ice cream." Eva chuckled at the dawning comprehension on the faces around her.

"All of this was because we decided to reward people with brown eyes."

Danni closed her green eyes in relief.

"When we single out certain groups for reward or for blame, that's prejudice. And when we see the young people we are working with as 'those kinds of people,' that's also prejudice. Whenever we have a preconceived notion of how a certain person is supposed to look, act, or even think, based on what they look like or where they're from, that's prejudiced thinking. Today, I hope that you have all learned something from this experience—I hope you've learned enough to never, never inflict this kind of hurt on anyone else.

"For every one of you in this room who felt hurt this past week, I'm sorry. It has been a hard lesson to teach. Those of us who were in on this had a hard time liking ourselves during all of this time." Eva's eyes filled with tears and she paused, blinking hard.

"I'd like to say something," a voice from the back spoke up. Danni turned to see Perry standing.

Eva gave him a teary smile, and nodded for him to continue.

"I'd like to say that this was the hardest thing that I have ever had to do to anyone," he said, his voice quavering. "Some of you made it pretty easy to pass you over and tell you that we were out of ice cream, because you didn't care, or you believed me. But some of you—" he shook his head.

"I felt like such a jerk looking at the hurt on people's faces. People who were nice people got passed over, just because of the color of their eyes. It made me realize how stupid and hurtful prejudice is. And let me tell you, I'll never judge someone by how they look again, with God's help." He sat down.

"I want to say that I'm proud that I have the chance to work with such quality people at Lupine Meadows," Lee Macomber commented. "I know that God has been using us this summer, and will continue to."

Mr. Ahrens stood up. "People, this has been a difficult week. For some of you, it has been even harder, because you knew this was wrong, yet you could do nothing about it. When we work with these kids next week, you will find some of them are bitter and hard because they have been dealing with this all of their lives. If we are Christian people, we have to be different. As people of God, we should conduct our lives in such a way that prejudice and racism have no place in our thoughts and in our actions. Think about that this week, and let it change you. Let's close this portion of our meeting with prayer, then get down to planning."

As the staff filed through the lunch line in the cafeteria, Roseanne joked, "Well, at least we know Perry won't hold back on the ice cream ever again."

"I know he won't give me any today," Danni said. "We didn't have it for a meal last week, and you know all we eat on Sundays are leftovers."

"It's just like home," Darla groaned dramatically.

The four girls laughingly made their way toward a table.

"Danni! You forgot something!" She turned toward the voice. Perry hurried after her with a bouquet of flowers in his hand.

"These are for me?" Her brows arched.

"If you'll still be my friend," he grinned. "Deal?"

"Deal." She gave him a bear hug. "You're the best."

Perry waved to Darla, Roseanne, and Lena, and hustled back into the kitchen.

"Nobody else got flowers," Lena batted her eyes.

"Don't start," Danni warned, hugging her flowers to her.

Maybe it would be a good week after all.

CHAPTER 9

Rainy Day Blues

"This is *not* the best time for this to happen, Lord." Eva looked up at the gray clouds boiling across the morning sky and spoke earnestly to God. "I don't know what to do with 200 inner-city kids in a rainstorm. I need them to be outside, running around. What are we going to do with them now?"

The side door to the program office blew open, and Lee Macomber and Danni flew in.

"Who ordered this?" Macomber rubbed her arms briskly to warm them.

"I don't know—all I know is that if we don't do some fast revamping, these kids are going to get bored. And when they get bored, there's trouble." Eva shook her head and sat huddled at her desk.

"We've got a heater in here somewhere . . ." Danni rummaged in a storage closet, found the heater, and plugged it in.

"At least we've still got power," Macomber said.

"Take that back, Lee!" Eva cried. "Don't even think it! Just what we need—175 girls with no way to blow-dry their bangs."

"The natural look is in," Danni snickered.

Eva rolled her eyes. "Where's our able leader and his spouse?"

"They'll be here as soon as they can . . . there was a little altercation at breakfast, and Mr. A has had to take a little time to settle it."

Danni sighed. It was a bad time for rain.

"What can we do inside that's fun and that everyone will participate in . . ." Macomber mused. "I know. Let's have a party."

"What kind of party? I have a Luau planned for this week because we're going to spend a day at the lake. I won't have time to do much shopping for anything else."

"I know," Danni blurted, "a sock hop!"

"A 1950s party?" Macomber asked.

"Yeah, complete with a dinner, music, entertainment—the works!" Eva now caught her enthusiasm. "And we won't have to decorate much."

"We have in the costumes department a few pairs of roller skates. Why don't we find the best skaters in the bunch and have them serve the kids on skates. We can have a costume contest, have prizes, and maybe play something else . . ." Danni was getting ideas faster than her hand could scribble them down.

"Mr. A could lead a march," Macomber suggested.

"A march?" Eva and Danni looked at her.

"Oh, you're making me feel my age," Lee groaned. "Eva, didn't your parents square dance or something?" Eva raised a quizzical brow. "Oh, never mind, I'll just tell you," she went on. "It's like a couples 'Simon Says.' Mr. and Mrs. A will start out walking together to music, and all of the couples will line up behind them. The object is to do exactly what the Ahrenses do, no matter what, and stay in step with the music."

"Why don't we just play 'Simon Says'?" Eva chuckled.

"Because this is more fun," Lee Macomber assured her. "Let me ask the Ahrenses. I'm sure they'll say yes." She floated out the door.

87

"OK, one evening down, how many to go?" Eva groaned.

The storm broke just after lunch. Campers went shrieking back to their cabins as the rain sheeted down, and the thunder rolled. They spent the Quiet Hour (renamed the Social Hour in honor of the teens) playing board games and drinking hot chocolate.

Danni frantically manufactured signs and posters and taped them to windows and tacked them under dry overhangs.

"'Let's go to the Hop'?" one boy read skeptically, stepping out of the rain. "What's a hop?"

"It's what you make beer out of," the boy next to him snickered.

Danni hesitated, then stopped. "It's a party," she called back to them, then continued on her way.

"Are we having beer there?" the boy hollered back, elbowing his companion.

"Root beer," Danni replied with a grin, having had the last word.

Back at the program room Eva fussed around with the pens on her desk. "Hey, boss, you look really busy," Danni teased as she shucked off her jacket and cap. "What have you got in line for the afternoon?"

"I don't know . . . the outdoor classes have to be cancelled—I mean, there's no way anyone can ride horses, shoot archery, play baseball, swim, or anything in this." Eva closed her eyes.

"At least we have the arts and nature building," Danni shrugged.

The door blew open again as Macomber entered, looking drowned. She wiped at the straggling curls plastered to her face and grinned. "You're never going to believe this," she chortled.

"Oh, let me guess," Eva interrupted dryly, "the Ahrenses are really gung ho about the whole thing."

"Of course, and there's more," Lee smiled. "I announced the First Annual Rainy Nights Lip Sync Contest to each of the cabins. Everyone is now practicing for their lip sync and putting together their outfits."

Eva sat up, looking interested. "What could we give as prizes for that?" she muttered to herself, narrowing her eyes in thought.

"The kitchen okayed the change in menu for tonight, so we will be having burgers and fries. Some of the extra staff will have to man the blenders for shakes, though. The kitchen kids will have a lot to do," Lee continued.

Eva nodded to herself in agreement, then bent and scribbled a few words on a piece of paper. "*This* is a woman in the midst of a brainstorm," Danni chuckled to Macomber.

"Oh, no, she gets worse," Lee replied, smiling. "You'll see."

Eva jumped up. "Wait!" she cried out to no one in particular. "Oh, no! Poor David! He's going to be swamped this afternoon. I've got to . . ." she struggled into her coat without finishing her sentence. Danni looked at Lee and shrugged.

"Have you got the signs all up?" Eva asked over her shoulder.

"Y-e-e-s." Danni gave her a distrustful look.

"Great. Come on. Idea. We don't have much time." She motioned for Lee and pulled Danni, coatless, out of the door.

Two hours later Danni slumped in exhaustion at a table. The sound system was set up, the skates had been located, and the available staff had each had a whirl around the waxed floor of the cafeteria. Danni was grateful that they hadn't expected her to help serve.

"We'll let some of the others do that," Eva had told her in the middle of directing traffic. "I need you to run errands."

And *run* she had. Danni had a stitch in her side from her frequent trips between the program room's costume basement and the cafeteria. She put her head down on her arms and took a moment to rest. "A real taskmaster, isn't she?" a voice said over her head.

Danni just groaned in response. "You don't know the half of it, David," she wheezed without lifting her head.

"Well, here." He pressed something cold and hard against her arm. "I brought you both a soda. If I can just get her to sit down and drink it . . ."

"Good luck," Danni laughed, sitting up. "She hasn't stopped for anything yet."

He frowned down at her. "Not even for lunch?"

"She had some orange juice or something in the program room because she didn't feel like going out in the rain . . ." Danni trailed off uncertainly at the expression on his face.

He picked up the other soda he had set on the table and with a curt "Excuse me" strode rapidly across the room toward Eva. "Oh my," Danni murmured and stood, her mouth open in surprise.

From the determined set of his shoulders, she could see that David was a man with a mission. He waited quietly next to Eva as she finished giving instructions to Jon and Lisa from the kitchen, then, as she turned to him, he put his arm around her shoulders and propelled her rapidly toward the door. "What are you doing?" she heard Eva ask in alarm.

"We're having lunch," David responded firmly.

The door closed on her protests.

Danni closed her mouth, then smiled dreamily. Really, it was too perfect. Hyperactive Eva and solid, dependable David. She sighed as she stepped away from the table, turned, and ran right into Perry.

"You see the happy couple too, eh?" his mouth quirked into an oddly bitter half smile. "It's too bad she doesn't have any time for him."

"What? What do you mean she doesn't have time for him? I've seen her around him; she likes him—I think," she hastened to add.

"Yeah, well, she sure doesn't act like it," Perry griped. "My brother Joel is David's roommate back at college, and he says that Dave's been after her all year. She is just too busy running everything."

Danni's brain went blank for a moment. She couldn't imagine what was making him sound so angry. "Running everything?" she blurted.

"Pretty much the whole school. Apparently David just doesn't have the right stuff for the little woman." His voice had a jeering note.

"Watch it, Perry," Danni warned. "She's my friend."

"No, I'm serious," he protested. "She is on every committee at school, she serves on the student senate, she's on the paper, she's in two choirs—"

"That's what you're supposed to do in school, experience everything," Danni broke in to defend her friend. "I'm involved with a lot too."

"But you would know how to make time for me, or I wouldn't be with you," he shot back.

The words hung in the air between them. Perry's face looked flushed. He muttered, "Gotta get back to work," and, squeezing her shoulder, hurried away.

Danni felt deflated. There was still no sign of Eva returning, so she walked slowly out of the cafeteria.

A light rain still fell. The sky looked gunmetal gray and depressing. Only the wild flowers on the meadow floor seemed oblivious to the showers. Danni went to find Gloria. She would know the scoop on the whole thing.

CHAPTER 10

The Heart of the Matter

Danni found Gloria in her room, pinning up her dark hair. "Hey, *hermanita* (little sister), where's your outfit?" she asked around a mouthful of pins.

With a shrug Danni sat down at her desk.

"You seen Eva?" Gloria watched her in the mirror.

A shake of the head. "David Taylor took off with her."

Gloria's brows arched and she spit out her pins. "Tell!" she demanded, plopping down on the bed.

"Perry seems really mad about it, and he's not even involved," Danni finished. "I think he and his brother have tried to talk David out of this, or something."

Gloria looked pained. "This is not working," she said quietly, picking up her pins. Willing Gloria to continue, Danni sat still a moment.

"Danni, it's not my story to tell you, so I won't. But . . ." She fidgeted with her pins, then put them down again.

"Maybe I'd better go."

A shake of the head. "Eva should be here any minute if she's going to put on an outfit before dinner. She probably just went somewhere to be alone."

"Well, I don't want to bug her," Danni hedged, suddenly wanting to escape the sadness in the other girl's voice.

"I think she needs to hear this." Gloria said the words slowly to the opening door.

"What now?" Eva asked dully, shuffling into the room.

"I was just—" Danni suddenly felt at a loss for words as she looked at her friend. Eva's face was streaked with rain and tears and her dark eyes were swollen.

"So what is it, what blew up, what else went wrong, are we having snow?" Eva turned a twisted smile to Danni.

The younger girl shook her head mutely.

"Good. Now I can lie down and die in peace." She sank down onto her bed.

"Did you throw up?" Gloria asked in a soft voice, bringing her roommate a warm towel from the bathroom.

"Nothing to throw up," Eva barked a harsh laugh and covered her face with the towel. "I think I finally convinced him this time," she said in muffled tones.

Gloria shook her head. Danni stood up quietly and edged toward the door.

"Don't ever fall in love," Eva said, wiping her eyes.

"But he likes you," Danni protested.

"His family doesn't." Eva blew her nose decisively on a wadded tissue she pulled from her pocket. "I got a visit last year from a very well-dressed matron who counseled me on the error of getting involved with any young man too soon in my college career. She let me know that she would 'take steps' to ensure her son's success in college, and that she was sure I understood."

"His mother?" Danni stared in horror.

"The one and the same," Eva smiled through her tears.

"What did he do?" asked Danni.

"Nothing. Because she never told him," Gloria snapped.

"What? Why?" Danni turned toward Eva.

"Because it really isn't about his schooling." Eva caught Danni with her eyes. "It's about them having money and prestige in the community, and about them hoping someday to have an important son. Do you understand that I don't fit in with all of that, that I don't want to take what could be his life away from him?" She searched the younger girl's face.

Danni shook her head speechlessly, tears in her eyes.

"But you're not being fair," Gloria cried softly. "David's a friend of mine, and I see you both suffering. You aren't giving him any credit for being a person of integrity. Can't you see that this is hurting him more than knowing what his mother has done?"

Eva shook her head stubbornly. "Glory, don't start, please. Don't."

Danni looked at her hands. As she studied the tanned, freckled skin covering them, she was more conscious of her skin color than she had ever been before in her life. Hesitantly, she reached out her hands to Eva and placed them on the girl's face, admiring the dark skin contrasting with the light. The words forced themselves out of her before she could stop herself.

"Don't ever let anyone tell you that you aren't a beautiful, special person," Danni said with a wobble in her voice. "Take it from a White girl."

Eva reached out and hugged Danni to her. Gloria stood and hugged them both. "If it's to be, the Lord will make a way," she said.

They stood a moment, sniffling, drawing strength from their friendship. Then Eva broke the silence. "What time is it?"

"Oh, no, here we go," Gloria complained.

"We have 20 minutes before the program starts," Danni wailed.

"Wear something of mine," Eva and Gloria responded in unison, then laughed. Their laughter made them forget the pain of their problem for a time, but Danni prayed quietly in her heart that she would be able to do something for Eva.

CHAPTER 11

A Cry From the Heart

The party was a roaring success. Roller-skating waiters and waitresses glided through the room bearing trays full of burgers and fries. The lip sync contest took place as the meal wound to a close. Danni grabbed a chair at the back of the room and watched the contestants.

"Now, that guy scares me," Gloria muttered around a mouthful of burger. "Look at him! He really looks like Elvis!"

Danni laughed. "Elvis Costello, maybe. What's that dance move he's trying to do?"

Gloria shook her head. "I don't know, but for his health, I think he should stop. He's going to hurt himself."

Clapping and bouncing in her seat to the music, Danni enjoyed the contest. Eva went on stage to announce that the judges would confer to decide the winner. It took everybody by surprise to hear someone shout "Wait!"

All eyes turned to see a group of staff making their way to the makeshift stage. Danni saw that it included Perry, Jon, Kevin, Darren Irwin (the boys' director), and David. Eva gave them a nervous glance. "Well, what'll it be, gents?" Lee Macomber called from her spot at the sound system.

Jon said the name of some song, but so softly that Danni did not hear it. The tune, though, was familiar. Gloria poked Danni. "'Since I Lost My Baby,'" she whispered. "Wonder whose idea that was?"

Danni shook her head and watched Eva, who looked as if she wished she could sink through the floor. Danni smiled as she heard the chorus. The applause was deafening after the staff group finished. They took their bows, David not looking in Eva's direction at all. As they left the stage, Jon's deep bass led the group as it broke into an impromptu rendition of "Good Night, Sweetheart." Eva took the mike, grinning.

Danni took advantage of the moment. "Gloria, what did Eva say to you about not talking to David about what his mother did?"

Gloria looked over at her and frowned. "She just said, 'Don't ever.' Why?" She peered suspiciously at her.

"Because I'm just wondering how much leeway I have."

Gloria's eyebrows jumped. "Danni, you might want to be really careful."

Waving her hand, Danni cut her off. "Glory, I know. Do you think I want to die? I know that this kind of thing always backfires. But I just want to do what I can to make sure that he doesn't lose hope. We can do that, can't we?"

"Who's *we?*" Gloria leaned away from her. "I don't know anything about any 'we.'"

Danni just smiled.

CHAPTER 12

Perseverance

The weather had cleared up by the next day, and the whole camp breathed a sigh of relief. The cabin areas returned to normal with festive banners of drying beach towels draped over the back porches. The arts and crafts building resumed normal operations as well, and Danni found David back at his pottery wheel.

"Hi," she greeted him, panting only slightly as she crunched up the remaining few feet of the pine needle covered trail.

"Well, hi yourself, stranger," he replied, his tired eyes lighting up. Danni noticed the weariness in his face. "Your boss lady finally giving you a moment of peace?"

"Actually, I'm stealing a moment," she stalled, glancing around. Suddenly she felt unsure of what she was about to do.

"Well then, I'll stop a moment too." He wiped his hands on a rag and stretched his arms over his head.

"How's your week going?"

He shrugged. "Just glad the rain stopped."

She nodded. "Me too. Eva was going out of her mind."

He looked down and began to pick the clay out from beneath his nails. "Yeah."

Danni felt her throat tighten. Suddenly she knew

that she had no business trying to interfere. But it made her hurt to see David looking so depressed. She found her voice. "Well," she said in a rush, "I just wanted to say thanks for bringing me the soda yesterday, and I just want to say don't give up too easily." She started abruptly for the trailhead.

"Wait. What?" He looked at her strangely.

"Don't give up," she called to him again, and started running, suddenly fearful of having to explain herself.

He stared after her for a moment, trying to understand what had just happened, then shook his head. "Guess my break is over," David muttered to no one in particular, and bent back over his wheel.

At lunch Gloria grabbed Danni's arm and hustled her over to the juice dispenser. *"What* did you say to David this morning?" she hissed.

"N-nothing," Danni stuttered, panicked.

"No, you said *something,"* Gloria insisted, filling a glass with fruit punch and smiling at a camper who came by to get some grape juice. As the young person walked away Gloria turned back to Danni. "Tell!"

"Honestly, I just said not to give up."

"You what?"

"Shhhh!" Danni darted a glance around the cafeteria. So far, no one had noticed their conversation. "I just said, 'Don't give up.'"

"In general?"

"In general. Like, 'Don't give up on anything in life'—you know?"

Gloria nodded. "Good. Simple, but good."

"Good?" Danni felt the beginnings of relief stirring in her.

"Yeah, great. You should see him. He's in a fabulous mood, and he said it was all because of you."

"Me?" Danni gave her an incredulous look.

"Yes, you," Gloria said a little sternly. "That's why I had to know what you said. We have to be careful not to give him false hope."

Danni shook her head. "I'm not giving him anything. I don't even want to say anything else to him. I never realized how serious people's feelings can be. He looked awful this morning."

Gloria nodded. "But, Danni, you know what he said? He said that you came along and gave him encouragement when he needed it, even though you didn't know he needed it. He said you helped him keep going."

"So God used me to help David even when I was going to be a busybody."

"You know what the Bible says: 'All things work together for good,'" Gloria reminded her.

"Yeah." Danni nodded, suddenly struck by an idea.

"Where are you going?" Gloria blurted as she waved to her and started out of the cafeteria door. "You didn't finish your food!"

"Gotta run!" she called back.

July 24 . . . Wednesday

Mi Familia, (See? I'm learning Spanish here!)

So much is happening. We're in the middle of inner-city week. Already it's rained, two kids thought that they were really good horseback riders and fell off, at least 10 people have been dunked in the horse trough, and one guy broke his arm at the nature center (hanging off the telescope tower!). Two cabins got KP for having a waterfight indoors, there was a pair of shorts on the flagpole . . . and it's only Wednesday!

I'm having a blast, though. It's been fun to get to work everywhere. I helped serve in the cafeteria on Tuesday night when we had carnival night. That was Eva's day off, which she really needed. She's started to look a little frayed around the edges, if you know what I mean. I think everybody's tired, because no one goes to bed at a decent time this week. All of the counselors have to stay awake for a while to make sure that no one goes out to meet anyone else, and Lee and Darren Irwin (he's the boys' director) are going crazy.

That's kind of why I made everybody—even Kat Armstrong—a care package yesterday. I took quotes and scriptures that I have pasted in the back of my journal and wrote them on little pieces of paper with a little sketch on them, then I put one in everybody's mailbox. It's been fun to see what happened next. People are starting to get every-body little gifts. Eva brought back taffy from her day off and put a few pieces in everybody's mailbox. Perry—you re-member him—made little bitty cookies and wrapped them in foil. Kevin and Roseanne went in together on a big box of chocolates. It's nice to get encouragement you can eat!

And now, I have a few quotes for you.

"Hitch your wagon to a star."—Ralph Waldo Emmerson

"Never, never, never, never, never, never, never give up."—Winston Churchill

"This is the best summer I have ever had."—Me

Thanks for the new pad and pens you sent. I'm going through paper like—well, like it grows on trees! Tell Autumn hi, if you see her.

Love to all,

Danni

CHAPTER 13

One Day at a Time

"Hey, where've you been lately?" Danni's voice carried above the slap of jump ropes and jumping feet.

"Around." Perry sat down on the picnic bench next to her and watched the activity about them. "How do they do that?" he marveled, watching a tall, slender girl do a dance step and turn around while jumping between two ropes.

"Practice," Danni laughed. "The same girl has been trying to teach me since after lunch, but I keep falling when I try to jump in with her. Go, Angelique!" She waved a hand to the tall girl who waved back and executed another turn.

"So where's 'around'?" Danni turned back to Perry.

He grinned. "Back to the subject, huh? I went home for a day."

She nodded. "Hope everything's OK."

"Yeah, my folks are fine. I went to see my brother."

She studied his face, trying to determine whether she should ask anything further. He solved her dilemma by continuing. "My brother is getting ready to take off on vacation with some friends of our family, so I thought I'd see him off."

She raised her eyebrows questioningly at him.

"He's coming up here today to see if he can't talk Davy into going with him."

"What?" she coughed. "What'll we do for a crafts director?"

Perry pounded her on her back. "Mrs. A can manage," he assured her.

She winced away from his pounding. "I'm sure she can. But does she want to?"

Perry eyed her cautiously. "She will when he tells her he's taking David for his own good, no offense."

Danni sat with her lips pursed for a long moment, fighting the urge to snap at him, then took a deep breath. "You guys are really caring friends," she said tersely, "but David probably won't go with you because when he starts something, he finishes it." She stood.

"You're probably right," Perry admitted with a shrug, "but Joel and David's mom thinks it'll be worth a try."

She frowned. "I've got to go, Perry."

He slumped dejectedly. "You're always busy," he accused only half teasingly. "Eva's had a bad influence on you."

Danni stiffened. "Would you lay off Eva already?" she snapped.

Perry threw up his hands in defense. "Hey, I'm joking, I'm joking," he protested.

"It's not really funny," she replied a little stiffly. "That kind of stuff can hurt people's feelings."

He shook his head. "You're too sensitive."

Danni rolled her eyes. "Whatever. See ya." She ambled casually off in the direction of the nurse's station, inwardly raging to herself.

"Gloria," she burst out as she saw her friend, "do you have a second?"

"In just a minute I will. I have one shot to give, and then I'm through with routine stuff for the afternoon.

Do you guys need some help in programming?"

"No . . . but who do you have to give a shot to?" Danni looked nervous.

"One of our campers this week is a diabetic who doesn't like to shoot his own insulin. At home his mother does it, and I'm taking care of it for him this week."

"Ouuuch." Danni made a pained face. "I'll be in the waiting room."

Presently the door opened and a young boy walked out, followed by Gloria. Danni looked at him, wide-eyed. He caught the expression and laughed. "It's not that bad," he reassured her with a smile.

"Wanna come up?" Gloria said. "I was just going to change and run over to the crafts building to put a coat of glaze on my watermelon pot."

"Uh, yeah. I don't have great news for you."

"Oh?"

Danni quickly related what she had learned.

"Hmmm." Gloria crossed her arms and looked up at the ceiling. "Where is Eva?"

"She was just finishing lunch. I know this afternoon we're supposed to be taking some pictures for the Saturday night slide show, so she'll be heading downstairs for a camera."

"I think that she should start shooting at the crafts building." Gloria took off her white coat and laid it over her arm.

"I'll be right back," Danni said.

"It is nicer to shoot here in the afternoon," Eva exclaimed. "The lighting is a lot better—not so harsh. The woods give this place a lot of subtle coloring that you can't get in the morning." She frowned as she looked ahead on the trail. "Did the Ahrenses get a new car?"

"Not a gray sports car," Gloria said.

"Maybe there are parents visiting." Eva patted her hair. "Let's get on our PR faces."

"Yeah, right," Gloria said. "You've been mistaken for a camper twice this week."

"Don't remind me," Eva groaned.

They entered the crafts building by the side door. Mrs. Ahrens, in a paint-splattered apron, greeted them as they came in. She moved closer to them and spoke in a low voice. "If one of you wouldn't mind helping me out for a few minutes, I'd really appreciate it. David's family came by, and there seems to be some sort of tension. I'd really rather not bother him, but Eva, could you help out?"

"Wh—yes." Eva was floored. "Is that who the sports car belongs to?"

Mrs. A nodded. "Apparently some of Perry Bowman's family are here as well. I've heard that the families are good friends."

Danni picked up Eva's camera in sweaty hands. "Why don't I take a few shots while you guys do your thing?" she suggested.

"Good idea," Mrs. Ahrens nodded to her.

Danni moved toward the back of the room and took a moment to look at the many projects covering the back table. The kids had made clay refrigerator magnets in the shapes of geckos, bunnies, and clouds. Decorative mugs and candleholders lay next to plaster cherubs painted white and gold. Danni took a few shots of the angels, and was admiring the glass paintings when the back door opened. A tall woman with carefully coiffed and frosted blond hair piled on her head glided through the door, followed by David and another boy Danni didn't know. Danni couldn't keep her eyes off the woman. Her resemblance to David, although slight, was noticeable in the piercing intensity of her eyes. Danni shrank as those eyes pinned hers.

Following his mother's glance, David smiled at Danni. "Mother, this is my friend Dannielle. Danni, my mother, Edith Taylor." Mrs. Taylor inclined her head only the slightest bit.

He continued. "This is Gloria Rodriguez, our nurse; Mrs. Ahrens, our director's wife and my assistant; and Eva Davies, my—" he stumbled, "our program director here and my friend."

Mrs. Taylor had favored everyone with an unsmiling but gracious nod, but her head swiveled as she saw Eva. High color filled her face, and her eyes took on a dangerous glitter.

"Eva, how have you been?" she asked in a clear alto voice.

"Just fine, thank you." The girl's jaw was clenched.

"You've met?" David was speechless and looked from one woman to the other.

"Just on one, memorable occasion," Eva smiled politely. "Excuse me." She dusted off her hands and turned to walk into the storeroom.

"Wait a minute, Evie. Would you come outside for a moment?" David's brow furrowed as he looked at her. She turned and gave him an odd look. "Just for a moment," he requested.

"David," his mother began.

"Excuse us," he said curtly, and ushered Eva outside. His mother, after a bewildered pause, followed. The boy who had come in with them shrugged, turned, and went outside as well.

Gloria painted a final coat on her jar and set it aside, then stood to help Mrs. Ahrens with some of the clean-up chores she was doing. As she walked past Danni, she whispered, "Pray."

Danni carefully took pictures of various campers, all the while listening with half an ear to the voices outside.

She heard the car pull off and drive away, and her stomach knotted. Did David go with them? She resisted the urge to peer out of the dusty window.

"Take a picture of this," a camper urged her, and she turned toward him to do that when the door squeaked opened. Heart in her throat, she turned, camera trained. She was blinded by Eva's smile.

"By no means does it mean 'happily ever after.' " Eva couldn't keep the grin off her face. "But it does mean that at least we're free to be friends now."

"*Good* friends," Gloria snickered. "Good, good, *good* friends," she chortled.

Eva threw a pen at her. "Quiet, you," she said good-naturedly.

"What a relief," Danni said. "His mother looks positively icy! How did she take you telling him what happened?"

"She just looked straight through me." Eva sighed. "I'm afraid that I'm never going to be friends with her. She's just too afraid."

"Afraid? I—she—she's afraid of what?" Danni was confused.

Gloria turned to her. "Prejudice is fear—sometimes fear of the unknown, or of what you don't understand. Mrs. Taylor doesn't know anything about Eva except that she's from a vastly different cultural background. Besides, if David dates Eva it would change the relationship between her and her son."

"But," Danni protested, "she wrecked the relationship between her son and herself by herself. She's the one who was meddling."

"True," Eva agreed, "but it's easier for her to blame me for that."

Danni shook her head. "It's really pathetic when parents want to control their kids that badly. Do you think that David and his mom will ever have a good relationship again?"

Eva sighed. "No. I used to be afraid of being to blame for that, too, but now I have to wonder if they ever had a decent relationship in the first place."

"Evita, that's not your worry," Glory said. "You just be there for your . . . *friend.*" She wiggled her eyebrows mischievously. "When he needs you. God will help him take care of the rest." Eva nodded her assent.

After supper that evening Danni sat on the cafeteria stairs, facing the sea of waving grasses and flowers on the meadow. A light breeze cooled her face, and the setting sun washed her in a peach-tinged gold. As she stared out into the end of the day, Perry sat down beside her. He bunched his apron up under his head and stretched out his legs.

"Still mad at me?"

She hunched a shoulder. "No."

"Joel came by before he left."

She nodded.

"Said it was a disaster."

She shrugged. "Was it?"

"Yeah, guess David's set on getting together with Eva whether anyone wants him to or not."

After closing her eyes briefly, she nodded.

"Danni?" Perry turned toward her seriously. "Do you think it's right?"

"Right?" Danni was confused at his tone. "What?"

"For him to date her. Her background is so different, and—" He broke off.

She faced him. "Perry, remember the eye thing? Maybe I'm not the right person to ask." Then she lurched to her feet.

Perry scrambled up beside her. "Don't get mad," he begged. "I'm not prejudiced against her—you know I'm nice to her, and she's a nice person. But isn't it just better if people stay with people like themselves? Danni, where are you going?"

"To find someone with green eyes—I should stick with my own kind, you know," she smiled sadly over her shoulder. "See you at campfire."

CHAPTER 14

The Beginning of the End

The buses pulled out of the lot packed with campers, some shouting out their goodbyes, others loudly singing camp songs and clapping.

"Hey, everybody, we did it!" Lee Macomber hollered enthusiastically. The staff applauded themselves as they thundered into the meeting room.

Danni grabbed herself a seat on the second row and scanned the crowd for Darla and Lena. She saw Katherine Armstrong's bright hair streak past her to the front row and craned her head to see where Kat was going. To her surprise, she saw her head for the empty seat next to David . . . the one that his arm was resting on.

"Stop!" Danni wanted to yell. "That's Eva's seat!" But she bit her lip and didn't say anything.

"Good morning, Dave," Kat purred as she sank into the chair. David removed his arm.

"Morning, Katherine," he said cheerfully. He turned around in his seat and, spotting Danni, said, "Would you mind lending me a seat from your row? I want to make sure and save a place for Evie."

Danni's face split into a grin. "Sure." She pushed a chair toward him. On the other side of him Kat sat very still.

The calm before the storm, Danni thought grimly. She waved Darla over to the seat next to her. Kat chose that moment to notice her. "Oh, hi, Danni," she chirped. "I haven't seen you around much lately."

"It was a busy week," Danni replied cautiously.

"I've seen Perry around Lena a lot," Kat continued innocently, "but not you. What happened?"

Danni sucked in a quick breath. Darla glanced at her. "I don't know what you mean."

"Oh, come on, everyone knows you two were an item. Did you have a little fight?" Kat baited her, eyes round.

Danni shook her head. "We were never an item, Kat. We're still great friends, but we're both just working hard. That's what we're here for." She shrugged and smiled, trying to figure out what the girl was up to.

Kat looked about ready to say more, but she stopped. Danni turned to see Eva wending her way through the crowd toward David's side. Danni glanced at him and saw that he was already smiling. She couldn't help joining him in a smile too.

Eva's keen eyes took in the chair situation at a glance, and amusement quirked her mouth. "Hi, Kat! I'm glad you're on the front row—I'm giving our devotional talk this morning, and I need someone to be my assistant. You're in the right place."

Red blotches suddenly spread over Katherine's neck. "I don't agree to helping you with anything unless I know what. And nothing that makes me look stupid!"

Eva's easy laugh was reassuring. "Now, Kat, would I do that to you? I just need you to hold a sign."

"OK," Kat gave in sullenly.

All throughout worship Danni chewed her nails and thought about Kat's comment. Ever since she and Perry had disagreed about Eva and David, she had avoided him. She decided to talk to Gloria about it that afternoon.

Work assignments found Danni not in the infirmary as she had hoped, but at the nature center to assist Glenda in cleaning out aquariums and terrariums. She hiked across the meadow bridge and up the steep hill toward the building. As she pushed open the heavy glass door, a still figure startled her. She had a moment's fright before she realized that it was a mannequin dressed in Native American clothes from a Plains tribe. She examined the exquisite beadwork in the leather shirt and moccasins. Glenda startled her again as she spoke from behind her.

"Pretty, isn't it? I like the headband the best." She pushed back her brown hair. "I could use one now."

Danni turned to smile at the quiet girl. "Are you up here alone? Where's Bill?"

"He got attached to one of the campers this week and rode shotgun on the bus to spend a little bit more time with him and meet his mother," Glenda replied.

"That's nice. I really liked a lot of the kids this week too."

"They just all think we're married," Glenda complained laughingly. "If I had a dollar for every time I had to correct one of the kids for calling me Mrs. Wright I'd be a wealthy woman!"

"Well, you guys do make a good team," Danni smiled. "Macomber says that it helps some of the kids to be able to think of us as stable parent figures—that way they feel like there is some safety in their world."

Glenda nodded and blew out a long sigh. "It's a hard world for some of them." Deliberately she changed the subject. "How's Kevin these days?"

"Kevin?" Danni gave her a bewildered look.

"Yes, Kevin. I thought that you guys were really close friends. Every time he comes up here he tells us what you're up to. He's a sweet guy."

"Kevin?" Danni squawked again. She thought of the quiet, blue-eyed boy in the baseball cap.

"Am I hearing an echo?" Glenda laughed, her own blue eyes crinkling in merriment.

"Glenda, I hardly ever see Kevin anymore," Danni sputtered. "I mean, he's around and stuff, but . . ." She shrugged in confusion.

"I don't mean to tease you about him; I just assumed he was a close friend of yours. I haven't seen him much this last week."

Danni shook her head. "No—I mean, yes. We're friends through Roseanne, but I hardly know him—I mean, not very well. It's not like I don't like him, he's nice, but . . . we're not that close," she finished clumsily.

"Well, forget I said anything," Glenda said hastily, waving her hands. "This is probably something else Bill mentioned to me that I should have forgotten about."

"He said something else?" Danni demanded. "What?"

Glenda laughed. "Nothing about you, my dear, don't worry." She placed her arm around Danni's shoulders. "Let's start with the reptiles."

For a while they talked of nothing but their work. A lizard escaped and led Danni on a chase through the reptile room, but the cold tile floor slowed its progress and finally they nabbed it under a workroom sink. When they had order restored, Danni carefully brought up a subject close to her heart. "Glenda, may I ask you your opinion?"

"Shoot," she said, pushing up her sleeves and plunging her arms into another tank. Lifting out a heavy snake, she checked his scales quickly for any parasites before transferring him to a temporary home. She glanced up at Danni. "Well?"

Danni chewed her lip. "Do you think it's OK for different kinds of people to date?"

"Different kinds?" Glenda rinsed out the snake's water bowl. "What do you mean? Rich people and poor people? Short people and tall people? Blond people and brunette people? Well people and sick people? Vegetarians and meat eaters?"

Danni heaved a sigh. "You know what I mean, Glenda."

"Yes, I do," Glenda grinned. "I just wanted you to hear how broad a question you actually asked."

Danni shrugged and replaced the lid on the terrarium she had cleaned. "I've never thought about it until a few days ago," she explained. "I didn't think it was a big deal, you know, but now I've heard from two different people that it's not something everyone thinks is OK." Perry's comments tumbled out.

Glenda replaced her snake and wiped her hands. "You know, I've known Eva since I was a freshman in college, and I've never seen her so happy in my life. How can that be wrong? No matter what anybody thinks." She leveled a serious look at Danni.

Nodding silently, Danni went back to work.

"Hopefully, this will be a normal week," Eva said as she brought her tray to the table. "I think I've had about as much turmoil as I can take for a while."

David dug into his salad. "We have only two more weeks of camp before the celebration," he said between munches. "What could go wrong?"

"Oh my, don't say that," Gloria sputtered. "If I thought it would help, I'd knock on wood."

David laughed, causing heads to turn all over the patio. Eva and Danni smiled, unable to help themselves at such an infectious sound. "Par*don*," David chuckled. "I keep forgetting your superstitious ancestry. Well, I don't think anything can go wrong. This has been the best summer I've ever had." He grinned at Eva.

113

Gloria rolled her eyes. "Here they go again."

"What celebration?" Danni asked, changing the subject.

"You'll see," Gloria answered.

"Unfortunately, you'll see more than I want you to," Eva lamented. "The celebration is supposed to be a banquet and awards ceremony for the staff at the end of the camp. Since this is your first summer, I wanted you to be able to enjoy it. But it's the evening when we work the hardest!"

"Sounds like I'll enjoy it. What kind of celebration are we having this year?"

Eva glanced narrowly at her. "Shh!" she hissed. "Not around outsiders!"

David and Gloria laughed uproariously. "Yeah, right. How long do you think it'll take me to get it out of her?" David said.

"You? *I'm* her best friend. She tells me *everything.*" Gloria fluttered her lashes. "Don't you, Evita?"

"I'm telling neither one of you anything," Eva scolded, reaching for a slice of melon from David's plate.

"Hey, there's a price for those!" David protested. "Information!"

"OK, I'll give you some info," Eva replied. "We're going somewhere on a day that ends in 'y.'" She smiled beatifically and took a dainty bite.

David looked at Danni. "I'm going to get it out of one of you," he said menacingly.

"Don't look at me," she said. "I just found out we have a celebration."

He grinned, flashing dimples, and pushed away from the table. "I've got to dash," he said to Eva, giving her a quick peck on the forehead. "Thanks for breakfast, everyone." He scooped up his tray and turned toward the dining hall.

Eva looked after him with shining eyes. "He is so

cute!" she sighed. "And I'm not telling him a thing." She took another bite of the melon slice and laughed.

"Will you tell me?" Gloria asked, scooting closer.

"As soon as I know," Eva promised. Gloria went away looking pleased.

"Are you really going to tell her?" Danni asked after Glory was out of earshot.

"Hmm. Just several different things. She'll have to guess which one is the truth." She took a quick sip of juice and looked at her watch. "Ready?"

"Sure." Danni scrambled to her feet.

August 3 . . . Thursday

Dear People:

OK, I haven't written in a while, and I'm sorry. Things got a little busy around here. I had a little accident while trying to get something from under my bunk. Hitting my head on the bedpost, I have the queen of all shiners. You would not believe the looks people give me. Gloria keeps telling me that she knows it was really Eva, trying to make sure I kept my mouth shut about the celebration week party. She's very sneaky, that girl.

Actually, on the serious side, we did have an accident today that kind of shook me up. My friend Bill Wright (nature center) and Kevin Birton (from church) went on a pack trip for a few days with the Mountain Lore camp. Bill usually takes a group by himself, but he'd been sick, and so took Kevin along for company and help. They were hiking up from some canyon, coming up the sheer wall of it, when some rock came loose. Kevin actually got buried in the dirt and pebbles that came down. By the time they had him out and worked their way up, it was getting dark. Since they didn't check in, Mr. Ahrens sent a tracking team after them. It's a miracle that he did, because Bill also was sicker than we thought. He had mono—and was dehydrated. He had to go to town to the hospital for a while and have IVs put into him.

The weird thing is that it made a lot of people say things that they didn't think they would ever say. Roseanne started crying out loud when she saw Kevin all scraped up and everything. Glenda went with Bill to the hospital—and on her day off. I visited Kevin in the infirmary, and he said he didn't think he'd ever been so glad to see me. Which is the weirdest thing by far that I've ever heard him say. Anyway, all's well that ends well, I guess. I cannot believe that the summer is almost over. It seems like I just got here.

Love,

Danni

CHAPTER 15

Celebration Week

"Hey, Perry," Danni greeted him as she sat in her usual spot on the picnic table. She hadn't seen much of him that week.

"Hey, Danni," he returned. "Catching some sun?"

"No, I'm just getting my fill of the meadow here. I can't believe that in just two weeks or so we'll be going home. I'm going to miss this."

Perry groaned. "Don't start with the 'missing' stuff already. I'm trying to figure out what I'm going to do for a job during the school year, and I can't think of anything as fun as this."

"I know. School will be so boring compared to this."

"What are you two sun worshipers complaining about?" Darren Irwin, the boys' director, stopped and thumped Perry on the back.

"We're just trying to figure out how to survive until next summer," Perry told him, shielding his eyes against the afternoon sun.

"Survive? Man, I'm so busy at school that camp seems like a vacation," Darren told them. "Aren't you guys involved with stuff like campus ministries, or the student association? Once you've worked here, you're in demand back at school. Don't worry guys, you'll be busy." He tweaked Danni's hair and took off whistling down the stairs toward the meadow.

"Hadn't thought of that," she mused, watching him go.

"Me neither," Perry responded. "That's actually a good idea. Maybe, with all of my kitchen experience, I can work at the food bank our church has. They have meals for the homeless every Sunday."

"Really?" Danni liked the idea. "Maybe our church has something like that. I'll have to find out if Roseanne and Kevin know. They're in the youth group." She stood up and stretched. "Back to work, I guess."

"Yeah." Hopping off the table, he gave her a quick hug.

"Thanks," Danni laughed, flustered. "I needed that."

Perry grinned. "Anytime, buddy." He loped back to the kitchen.

At supper Glenda cornered Danni. "Hey, girl, it's almost the end of the summer. When are you going to sleep out at the tower with me?"

Danni's eyes lit up. "Hey, I had almost forgotten about that. We've got the place to ourselves this time, right?"

"Right." Glenda grinned. "And maybe we can find Gaddabout and his mate. I'll check with Macomber. Meet me after campfire?"

"Sure!"

It surprised Danni later to see Glenda with her sleeping bag and a small backpack on her shoulders. "I thought we were just sleeping on the tower," she said, looking at the backpack.

Glenda grinned. "Well, Bill found out we were going to sleep out tonight and made some threats about paying us a little visit while we were snoring. I don't want to take any risks, so we're going to sleep out in the meadow tonight."

"What?" Danni felt both excited and dismayed.

"Yeah, there's a great camping spot complete with fire-bowl at the east end of the meadow. We can't get there by truck, so we're hiking in by moonlight. Still game?"

"Definitely."

"All right then." Glenda motioned her to the trail.

They walked for a ways in silence, Glenda using the moonlight to orient them along the trail. As they passed the baseball diamond, Danni remembered her first day at the camp when she had seen the staff playing ball. They walked farther into the tall grass, and Danni heard the movements of small animals. Once they even startled a hunting fox. As they drew nearer the tree line, the trail turned left. They entered the heart of the forest, and the lights of the camp dropped out of sight. Glenda took out her flashlight.

"It's harder to see by moonlight in here," she called back softly, "but we'll be there in a little while."

"Wait up," Danni said. "I can't see a thing!"

They stumbled along together, giggling when Danni tripped on a root and nearly pulled Glenda down with her, then shook with silent laughter when a hoot owl caused both of them to nearly jump out of their skins. Both were exhausted by the time they made it to the little camp. Glenda had laid the fire earlier, and now she lit it with a wooden match she pulled from the box in her backpack. Danni admired by the firelight the small clearing in the woods where they would sleep.

"It's really beautiful," Glenda agreed. "Just wait until morning when you see it."

"I think it's pretty now," disagreed a male voice.

Danni shrieked and jumped up from the log she was sitting on. Bill and Kevin came crashing through the woods from the other side of the fire. Glenda groaned.

"Oh, come on, you didn't think you'd get away from us *entirely*, did you?" Bill laughed.

119

"I was *hoping,*" Glenda said.

"Well, when we didn't find you at the tower, we figured that this was the next best place, didn't we, Kev?" Bill moved aside for Kevin to enter the circle of firelight.

Kevin looked down at the fire. "We brought you some chocolate," he offered.

"Great," Glenda said. "We have marshmallows. Too bad no one has graham crackers."

"Fingers will do," Bill reassured her. He went off to find some sticks.

"I also brought my guitar," Kevin said to Danni, his face shadowy in the firelight.

"Your guitar? You dragged *that* all the way here?" She was incredulous.

"Actually, we kind of cheated," Kevin grinned. "We drove in on the logging trail that's on the back side of the woods here."

"Well, go get your guitar and play something for us," Glenda urged.

Kevin shrugged and vanished into the woods.

"This is so nice," Glenda sighed, poking a stick into the crackling fire.

"You can really see the stars from here," Danni remarked, craning her neck to see the sky.

Kevin started to play "Twinkle, Twinkle, Little Star" on his guitar, and Bill groaned. "Don't do it, man," he threatened. "I didn't bring you out here to play nursery rhymes."

"What is your command, then?" Kevin bowed to him mockingly.

"Play that song you wrote," he suggested.

Kevin rolled his eyes. "Think again, William."

"I didn't know you were so musical," Glenda said.

"I'm not," Kevin replied. "I just like to pick up the guitar now and then." He strummed softly for a few moments.

120

"Is that the song?" Glenda asked.

"Nope."

"Ah, c'mon, Kev," Bill encouraged. "Danni, tell him you want to hear it."

She turned to Kevin. His hat was off, and a shock of blond hair hid his face as he bent over his guitar. "Don't play it if you don't want to," she said, smiling.

He looked up. "I'll play it for you," he said quietly.

Startled, she listened while he strummed for a moment. Kevin certainly had a lot of hidden talents. She was even more surprised when he cleared his throat and started to sing softly.

"How could I be so blind
 Not to see how your eyes shine?
 How could I see you smile
 And then walk away?

"How can my heart ignore
 All that I've been searching for?
 How could I be so blind—
 You've been here all the time."

"Kevin, that's beautiful!" Glenda exclaimed.

"I didn't know there were words to it!" Bill was floored. "Man, you are musical." He shook his head admiringly.

Danni could hardly talk. A million thoughts raced through her mind. She heard the words to the song echo around in her head. Finally she managed a "Wow."

Kevin ducked his head. "It's not finished," he said modestly. Then he straightened. "What time is it, Bill? It feels like it's getting late."

Bill groaned and stood. "It's pretty close to curfew. I'd better get you back."

Kevin picked up his guitar. "Too bad," he shrugged. "Well, good night."

Danni found her voice. "I'll walk you back to wherever."

"No, you'd better stay where you can see," Bill waved her back. "Buenas noches."

Glenda gave Bill a big hug. "Thanks for coming out, you guys."

"No problem," Kevin smiled. "See you tomorrow."

They walked off into the darkness with only a bobbing dot of light to show them the way. For a long time neither Danni nor Glenda spoke. They lay stretched out on their sleeping bags, each one content with her own thoughts and with the crackling of the fire. Finally Glenda broke the silence, humming Kevin's song.

"That was such a pretty song," Danni breathed. "I can't believe Kevin wrote a love song!" She shook her head in astonishment.

Glenda smiled from across the fire. "I can," she said. "I think he's in love."

"Really?" Danni surprised herself by feeling an acute pang of disappointment. "With whom? I wonder if Roseanne knows." She frowned to herself and stirred the fire with a stick.

Glenda sat up. "Danni," she said abruptly, "what do you think of Bill?"

"Bill?" Danni's thoughts derailed, then rearranged themselves. "I think he's great. He's a really good naturalist, he's always really nice to everyone, and he's kinda cute with those serious scientist glasses . . ." Danni stopped as lights came on in her brain. "Glenda, are you guys finally going out?" She sat up, peering through the firelight.

"No, no, no—nothing like that yet." Glenda raised her hands to ward off further questions. "I just thought I'd ask you, because . . . well, I have become rather attached to him this summer."

Danni remembered the time Glenda had spent with

Bill in the hospital and grinned to herself. "I don't believe what I think of him is the point," she laughed. "What do *you* think of Bill, Glenda? What does 'rather attached' mean, huh?"

"I think he's the nicest guy—I mean, he's a really Christian person, not just a religious one, you know? He does nice things, like going to meet Phan's mother after Inner-City Week. He didn't even think anything of it!"

"Those are the best kind of people," Danni agreed. "I hope I find someone like that."

"You will," Glenda reassured her.

"Of course I will. But *you've* found Mr. Wright!"

"Oh, go to sleep," Glenda said as she groaned at her pun.

"Good night," Danni chuckled.

It didn't seem like time was a ball rolling downhill to just Danni. David, in the arts and crafts building, started taking inventory of his supplies and complained that he would never finish before the week was out. Lee Macomber and Darren Irwin were doing staff evaluations as fast as they could. The camp store held a 50 percent off sale on just about everything. The cafeteria served leftovers almost daily. In programming, Eva was tearing her hair out to finish celebration festivities. Danni was feeling blue.

"OK, we can pack these costumes up since we won't be needing them again this year," Eva directed.

Danni took an armload of aprons and bonnets and sighed. "Eva, do you have to say that so cheerfully? I can't believe that this summer is almost over!"

The older girl laughed. "Well, Danni, we can't have summer forever. Don't worry. By this time next year you'll be in the swing of things more, and you'll be glad it's about over too."

"What do you mean?" Danni turned and faced her.

"What I mean," she said, looping an arm around Danni's shoulder, "is that next summer, if you're coming back, I'd like for you to be my full-fledged equal—my codirector."

"Really?" Danni's green eyes shone.

"If you'd like to."

"Eva, I'd *love* to!"

"Good," Eva said simply.

They went back to work, packing up costumes and taping inventory lists to the boxes they were in, cataloging props and makeup, and doing general repairs. As she packed each costume, Danni thought of the plays they had used it in, and the staff member who had worn it. She was nearly drowning in nostalgia when the door flew open and Kevin burst in, cap in hand.

"Guess what?" he blurted. "I'm going to be working with the horsemanship classes next summer. I'm going to be Jim Hodges' assistant."

"Really?" Danni jumped up and gave him a hug. "Good for you! And I'm so glad Jim will be back next summer."

"What about you?" Kevin twisted his cap between his fingers. "Are you coming back?"

"I never thought about doing anything else," she grinned up at him.

"Good." Kevin nodded, then reached forward awkwardly and squeezed her arm. He replaced his hat and added, "I can see you're busy. I just wanted to come by and tell you."

"OK," Danni replied, still feeling the pressure of his hand on her arm. "Thanks."

"Well, see ya." He ducked out the door.

Danni stood for a moment looking after him. Then she smiled. Suddenly the future seemed full of possibilities.

Lena made her way over to Danni's bunk, followed

closely by Darla and Roseanne. The trio deposited themselves on the floor next to the bunk.

"What's up?" Danni put down her sketch pad.

"I just talked to Macomber," Lena bubbled. "She's
doing staff evaluations, you know. I just got told that I
was going to be a substitute counselor next summer, if I
wanted to come back."

"Great! You'll have a different unit every day, right?
Talk about good experience."

Darla broke in, "I'm going to be a counselor next
summer. I'm going to have a cabin during 'disABILITY'
camp, and my sister is going to be here."

"You didn't tell me that, you bum," Lena
scolded, giving her friend a squeeze. "That will be
so fun for you two!"

"What about you, Roseanne?" Danni turned to the
petite blond. "Have you talked to Lee yet?"

"Not yet, but Kevin talked to Darren and found out
that he'll be working with Jim Hodges in horsemanship
next summer."

"He came by and told me," Danni replied, blushing.
Roseanne looked at her and grinned.

"Ten minutes 'til curfew!" someone yelled from
the doorway.

"I'd better get going." Lena uncoiled gracefully. Roseanne and Darla wished Danni a good night and followed.

Danni closed her sketch pad and stretched out on
her bunk. Almost before her head hit the pillow, she was
sound asleep.

The Camp Celebration was elegant and colorful. A
string quartet played classical music. Waiters glided by
with hors d'oeuvres and sparkling cider. Danni, Eva, and
Gloria surveyed the scene with satisfaction.

"It's nothing like you said it would be," Gloria

complained for the umpteenth time. "I dressed for a fiesta!"

"You look just fine," Eva laughingly soothed her friend. "You should know better than to trust what I say about celebrations by now."

Danni changed the subject. "Look at the flowers. Eva, everything looks great!"

Eva smiled modestly. "The crew did most of the work. Oh, looks like dinner will begin in a few minutes. Danni, do you have the awards ready?"

"Everything's right where you want it, ma'am. Everything will run smoothly, I promise."

"Great," Eva replied, already striding off toward the dining area. Tall David, in a dark suit and tie, trotted behind her, trying to keep up. Gloria shook her head smilingly.

"Gloria, can you believe we're on a boat?" Danni exclaimed in an awed whisper. They both peeked over the railing at the dark water rippling past the hull of the huge dining yacht.

Gloria shook her head. "She really outdid herself this time."

"She didn't even tell me," Danni complained. The two walked into the dining room. "Perry, you look great!" Danni exclaimed, seeing the dark-haired boy in a neat sports jacket and tie. "I can hardly recognize any of us without a pair of jeans on and a camp T-shirt."

"Well, you look gorgeous too. Green is really your color."

Danni shook her head at his silliness, then smiled as she watched him catch up to Lena and put a casual arm around her shoulders.

"This place is really something," Bill commented, appearing at her elbow. Startled, Danni turned around, nearly running over Glenda.

"Wow, look at you!" Glenda said. "You look so elegant

with your hair up! Did you and Eva do all of this work?"

"Thanks, you look great yourself," Danni replied, appreciating the contrast Glenda's crisp white suit made to Bill's navy blazer. "I hardly did anything. Eva cooked up most of this."

"Everything looks amazing. I wonder what we're having for dinner?" Bill sniffed appreciatively.

"Oh, come on, you," Glenda scolded, giggling. She dragged him toward a table.

Danni smiled as she looked around the room. Lee Macomber appeared relaxed and happy, joking with one of the girls from the kitchen. Mr. and Mrs. Ahrens had their heads together with Eva and were discussing something—probably the awards ceremony.

It took Danni a moment to realize that she was looking for someone as she smiled and chatted with her friends. By the time she finished eating her dinner, she realized who it was.

"Roseanne, did your brother come to the celebration?" Danni leaned across the table, frowning.

"He's around here somewhere," the other girl waved a hand. "You know how he is."

Danni excused herself from the table. As she left the dining room, she caught Eva's eye. "I'll be right back," she mouthed. Eva gave her an "OK" sign.

The deck was dim, and the night air was cool. Danni rubbed her arms as she walked along, peering into the darkness for a familiar face. The moon was rising, and she stopped for a moment to stare out into the water.

"Hi, Danni." Kevin materialized out of the darkness behind her. "I didn't know it was you."

"It's me," she replied, trying to see his face in the dark. "What are you doing out here?"

"Just looking at the water. The moon's really pretty, isn't it?"

"Yeah," she replied, looking up. "It's hard to believe that this is the last night everybody will be all together, isn't it? Here we've been practically living in each other's hair for the past 10 weeks, and now it's all over."

Kevin nodded and looked silently at the moon.

Faintly, Danni heard applause. A door opened, spilling light onto the deck in a golden pool. "Danni? Are you out here?" Eva peered into the darkness.

"I'm right here," she replied.

"You've won an award," Eva called. "The least you could do is come in and accept it."

Danni smiled. "I'll be right there," she called back. Turning to Kevin, she asked, "Are you coming in?"

He shrugged and smiled. "In just a minute," he responded.

"It's almost all over," Danni reminded him. She turned to walk away when Kevin caught her hand.

"Not everything is all over," he said, looking shyly into her eyes. "Some things are just starting." He looked at her solemnly, then moved close to her and touched his lips to her cheek. Danni stood, stunned, as he let go of her hand. She stumbled dizzily toward the door to the dining room. As she opened the door, her eyes took in all of the friends she had made at Lupine Meadows that summer. Bill, Glenda, David and Eva, Gloria and Darren, Lee, Perry, Darla, Lena, and Roseanne.

"This *is* just the beginning," she said to herself as she stepped into the brilliantly lighted dining room.